EMILY

EMILY
Or, the Voluptuous Delights of a Once-Innocent Young Lady

A Victorian Novel

ANONYMOUS

GROVE PRESS, INC./New York

First Black Cat Edition 1985

First Printing 1985

ISBN: 0-394-62069-0

Printed in the United States of America

GROVE PRESS, INC., 196 West Houston Street, New York, N.Y. 10014

CHAPTER 1

'You will marry soon', was often said to me at twenty, and so often that I began to think of marriage as a far-off country, or rather an island whereon the inhabitants would be vaguely strange to me—having other manners, other attitudes—and where mirrors (in rooms that I had not visited but knew I must encounter) would reflect different images of me to those with which I was the more familiar. Sometimes I thought of marriage as a chair, a high chair, high with a straight back, and having ornaments of pearls and plumes, and having crested arms, in which I would forever sit.

Such curious fancies often took me then, and still possess me of many other things, of customs, attitudes, and fancies eaten as one eats a small, sweet cake.

When I was young, was very young, in my eleventh year and still in bud, an old lady stopped me close by Shotter's Wood into which a meadow rises and disappears as if it had loped forward in a long, green wave and then had changed its mind, not wishing to disturb the saplings as they were then, long ago.

'Are there dreams to be had here, dear, my little dear?' she asked of me.

'Yes', I said—said 'Yes' in my simplicity, for I knew there were dreams in the myriad leaves, wound in among the stunted hedges, surging in the loam that flows like a dark sea among the aspens and the elder trees.

My aunt came hastening to me then, bidding a neighbour adieu, her footsteps purposeful along the lane. I felt her frown fall like a small cloud on my back.

'What is it that you want?', she asked the old lady

who mumbled something, turned, and went the way that she had come. I felt a sadness for her—black dress fading into horrid grey, perhaps a penny only in her purse.

'There *are* dreams to be had here, Aunty, are there not?', I asked.

'What nonsense! Is that what she told you, pray? Downcast are those who live in dreams, for few are ever realised. Examine your mind for practicalities. Absorb your five-times table, Emily.'

I did not, nor have done so since. Tradesmen count money; I do not. I count the pearls of precious moments, yes, small drops of sunlight that I keep among dried shells, old coins and broken necklaces. I count the kisses, quick, impassioned, I have known. Such are not practicalities, but needs.

Mama was not as my Aunt Mathilda was. When I spoke to her of dreams, she answered me in kind. Her lorgnettes would rise and she would peer at me with twinkling eyes.

'Absorb your dreams as earth absorbs the rain, and let them nourish you', Mama would say. My sister, Eveline, would use me as an echo-chamber at such times and afterwards would absorb the words from me. I was senior to her by three years and much her monitor in our beginnings. We have been fortunate that our thoughts breathe together, as the thoughts of sisters sometimes do. Our brother, James, was more independent in his ways at first, sought butterflies where we sought petticoats and thought himself a wild explorer with a telescope through which he would peer at other houses far away, across the valley where the sunlight drew long shadows on the grass.

'What do you see?' I asked him once, for I had tried it and the aperture seemed far too small for my quick eyes.

'He looks at the milkmaids', Eveline said. They

were known to piddle in the grass sometimes, and James had seen them do and said rude words of it, that he had seen their bottoms all a-gleam, that some wore stockings, some did not, but none had drawers they needed to pull down. We were heard to speak of drawers and such by Mama, but she did not mind. At this time I was near eighteen, and more in blossom than I knew myself to be in such male eyes as cast themselves upon my form.

Guests came and went like shadows then. They came from other worlds, I thought. The women all were pretty—some much younger than the men. I recall one, Adelaide, who was scarce much older than myself and sat with Papa and he touched her thighs. Her waist was wasplike, but no more than was my own. Her tutor, guardian—I know not who he was—sat next to me that evening. It was not our custom that the ladies should disperse from table that the gentlemen might smoke. Mama said this was a nonsense since the ladies then smoked, too, their gentle, perfumed cigarettes.

James, Eveline, and my elder sister, Jane, had gone to bed. I was the favoured one that night. Mama had a slight flush upon her cheeks at my continued presence, yet she let me stay. We having passed the stage of port and wine, I took to a liqueur, and found it creamy, heady—a delight. Across the table from me sat a girl of my own age. Her companion had a look I thought of then as saturnine. He held his arm about her waist and made her lean to him and kissed her neck. She stared up at the ceiling, blushed. I expected her to squeal, but she did not. Papa coughed—Mama made a clucking sound. I felt a hand upon my knee, and fingers groped my garters through my dress.

'We shall retire', Papa said, 'Let us to the drawing room'.

I made to rise. The hand up on my thigh prevented

me. Adelaide's guardian conveyed to me a winsome look. Chairs sounded in their scrapings and the others rose. In rising, others float when one is still. I felt transfixed. The hand soothed, found my stocking top, the nascent, glowing flesh above. 'Mama!', I wished to speak, but she had gone, the others in her train. The dining room enlarged itself, then shrank.

'Have you not been tutored?', I was asked. I strained my neck and stared at scattered plates, the debris of the feast, the wine stains on the otherwise clean cloth.

'Sir?' I spoke but did not look at him. His beard would graze my face, I thought. I moved my legs a trifle, felt his hand like a warm toad slide-slither down to feel my knees, then fall from me.

'Later, perhaps', said he, and rose. His hand extended to me. I was led into the drawing room. Mama gave a look, quick look, then motioned me to sit beside her which I gladly did. A couple sat upon the floor and kissed. Papa and Adelaide perched on a sofa a full foot apart like birds uncertain as to whether to roost or fly. Her corsage was undone. Her white chemise emitted spills of lace. Another couple were together in a chair, the female full upon his lap, a glass uncertain in her hand.

'There are times for dreams', Mama said, looked at me, then laughed self-consciously and looked away. Pamela, companion of the saturnine and older man, rose at a prod from him and came to me.

'We have nice things to show you in our room— my room', she said, correcting herself so quickly that the others laughed.

'I may to bed', I answered.

'No', Mama said, 'You may go and see, my pet— and then you may to bed. 'Tis early yet; you are allowed to stay up longer now'.

'I, too', the man said whose companion nestled the more deeply in his lap and whispered something in his

4

ear. The laughter there on bubbled all around, and Papa shifted close to Adelaide who gave me such a perky look and showed half of her titties, swollen, pale.

I did not look, I did not wish to look. I thought them all inebriated at the least, yet knew upon the very birth of that quick thought that it was false. There was a waiting for me to depart. I felt it like the chiming of church bells that come to one with vagueness on the wind and then retreat and fade and are not heard again.

The hall seemed hollow as we entered it. For the first time I had not kissed Mama, Papa, goodnight. I had my waist enfolded by the man. The girl preceded us. Her bottom swayed. Taller than I, she had long legs and showed a flash of patterned stockings, bootees black. Upon the landing, as we turned along the corridor, Eveline's door chinked open and she peeped, her nightgown swirling close around her thighs. Our eyes met, then she closed the door again. I knew exactly how she would lean against it, lean.

'A pretty girl', the man said, and he touched my bottom as he spoke. I felt myself urged forward to a further room, passing my own. The girl opened the door. As though I were in another house, I thought— as though I did not know the rooms that waited for their guests the long weekends. The bedclothes were drawn down; the sheet showed white, a waiting plateau, though I knew it not.

'We have time', the man said. There was awkwardness. I felt the awkwardness, but knew not what to say, but finally said 'Yes', I knew not why. The girl smiled, grateful for the word, and took my hand and led me to the bed. I felt as panicky as must a bird whose feathers are first clawed at by a cat.

'What is it you have?', I asked. I thought of ivory, of lace, of long and painted feathers, fans, some furbelows—I knew not what—and even so I knew they were not there.

5

'I shall to the water closet', said the man. The girl's grip tightened as he spoke. The door opened again and then was closed. I stood alone with her.

I turned, found myself turned, our faces close together.

'Kiss me', the girl said. There was urgency in that small voice. I had not kissed with lips to lips before and thought it strange a girl should want to do. I let her lips touch mine. How soft they were!—'No, *more*, you silly'. Her hands took my neck. Her mouth slurred the more closely into mine. Hands, arms, were twisted and I fell, fell falling on my back and she upon me with a little laugh, hands tight upon my shoulders so I could not move.

'Don't', I said feebly, but my mouth was smothered underneath her own. She groped my gown, began to draw it up.—'No, no—what do you do?' I blurted, felt her feel my thighs. She snapped my garters playfully and kissed my neck, forcing my legs apart to roll between, was heavy on me, breasts upon my own.

'He will birch me if I don't, and may birch you. Are you not birched?' she asked me. Her words spluttered on my lips.

'No please, get off. If Mama knows...'

'Your Mama knows'. The door re-opened and I heard his voice and saw the looming form above. 'Tell her that her Mama knows', he said.

'Of course, of course she knows. They are all busy downstairs, anyway', the girl said, mouth warm on my own.

'Let me get up!' I strained to force her off. At that, he fell beside us both and placed his stronger grip upon my arms.

'Take off her drawers and pleasure her', I heard. I squeaked, I kicked, I shook my head, hearing my own squeals—and yet I muffled them. Laughter and cries came faintly from below. I thought of Eveline and how

6

she often leaned against the bedroom door to hear the sounds that floated up on long weekends and how I wished that she would not.

My clothes thrown up, my bottom bumped. Ties of my drawers were loosed. I shrieked, whereat his hand clamped firm over my mouth. My drawers descended and were pulled right off, her shoulders forced between my thighs, knees on the floor as then she was.

Tip of her tongue—a stamen seeking me between my pouting lovelips.

'GOOO!' I choked. Legs quivering, I felt her find my spot and titillate it, tongue-tip swirling, moist. My tummy tightened and grew warm.

'Descending into pits of love'. His voice was husky to my ear.

Oh, I remember, I remember, yes, the curling shadows and the single lamp, the silence save for the warm hissing through my nose as her tongue lapped. My head sank back—his hand slipped from my lips. Unwanted were his lips upon my own, invasion of his tongue within my mouth. He held my chin to hold my mouth beneath. Oh yes—remembering how my legs strained, strained forward then, knees limp upon her shoulders and my toes a-curl in the first onrush of my spilling spurts.

'She is coming—coming on?' Raising his hungry mouth from mine, he held my shoulders down and turned his head.

'Mmmm . . . .', came her murmur.

'HAAAR!', I gasped. I arched my back. Her lips clamped to me suavely and her tongue still lapped, I spurting on—a fine rain in her mouth, and then, and then, my legs hung still and limp. Half closed as were my eyes, I saw the ceiling as a cloud. The house was not my own, no longer real.

'A fire will be lit in here in winter', the girl said. She rose and wiped her lips, then loosed her dress and

7

drew it off. Beneath, she wore only a chemise and stockings tightly gartered. The hem of the chemise swayed and flirted and I saw her bush. Placing his hands beneath my arms, limp arms, the man drew me up and sideways on the bed, my head upon a pillow, my dress rucked up the more, my belly shown.

'Remain so, for you look so sweet in disarray', he said.

'Me, too?', the girl laughed and she clambered over us and lay on the other side of me so that I then lay in between the pair.

'Mama...', I began. My mouth felt very soft. It was not a cry, but the beginning of an expression of belief that she might mount the stairs and intervene.

'Fires will be lit in many rooms tonight', the man said. Then he took my mouth. The girl caressed my thighs and fluffed my pubic hairs.

Once, I recall, when our carriage toppled, one wheel in a ditch and Mama screamed, I knew only the little world of the dust-hazed coach and its lopsidedness—knew only panic, fear. The world beyond had vanished. So it was within that bedroom then. The drawing room was part then of some otherness, as were the other rooms about the house. The gardens, dark with night, became a bog or a morass, perhaps. Fingertips soothed the innerness of both my thighs—eased them apart again.

'Make her come again', the man said, 'Let me watch her eyes'.

I bleated 'No'. Her mouth came over mine and then she slithered on to me again. 'No', I said 'No' again, but clutched her arms. Her stockings rasped to mine and then her bush purred moistly, stickily, to mine, and she began to move her hips and rub.

I heard my breath hurr deep into her mouth and clutched her arms. The bed bounced softly as we bumped.

8

'Do not!', my mind said, but I could not stop. Squirming of oily lovelips to my own, her belly warm and sleek to mine.

'Give me your tongue', the man said, and he took my face, brought it from under hers to gaze into his own. His hands cupped underneath my head. The breath kissed from my nostrils to his own. My knees pressed sideways, opened by the girl. Her breathing came as hurriedly as mine. The seconds passed; I stared into his eyes and through his eyes, my lips apart. He made me stay so, made me stay, watching the hidden flames behind my eyes. My belly tingled warmly and I felt her spurt her little rills of liquid round my quim.

'Emily—extend your tongue. Into my mouth. Now, do it, girl', he said.

'WHOO-AAAR!', I moaned. The white flames, small flames, 'flickers' (as I called them since) expanded in my honeypot, then held themselves as if within a ball, a sphere, that waits to burst. My corsage was un-buttoned as our mouths met in a sudden fury of desire, tongue long to tongue and wet and whirling round. My hand was taken, drawn down, grasped the root of him, thick root. I squeezed naively and I rubbed him there and felt him throbbing even more than I, his hand insurgent in my dress, my thorn-hard nipples stark against his palm. . . .

'He would have done it to me sooner if you had not brought him on', the girl said in our limpness after-wards. My hand was sticky from the stain that showed upon his trousercloth. The man lay still and sighed and stretched his legs.

'Mama may come', I said.

'She will not, but you seem to have a fear of it. How pleasant it was, though, was it not?', the girl said, warm thigh to my own, two pillows shared between the three of us.

'There will be fires lit in the rooms in winter', said

9

the man. He moved his hand, his knuckles to the wet-ness of my bush. I felt my tummy ripple to his touch. The girl moved slowly off the bed and slipped off her chemise. Her titties bobbled as she moved.

'You may watch us. Do you want to watch?', she asked.

'She cannot stay', the man said. He sat up, rubbed his face, then turned his body, kissed me on the lips. 'Already you have learned to wriggle and to kiss', he said.

'I cannot stay', I echoed, and my voice was like a piece of paper that lies blank, waits to be written on. Partly to my relief the girl moved round the bed and flung herself beside him. A possessive look was clear upon her face. I found . . . I found it difficult to move. They knew I found it difficult to move. The man lay back again. Both closed their eyes. The stain upon his trousers was a map of nowhere-nothingness, and yet was stark.

'Goodnight', I said. My voice rang hollow in the large, high-ceilinged room.

The door seemed heavier than I remembered all the doors. I heard them say 'Goodnight' and there was honey in the satisfaction of their tones.

Along the corridor I stopped at Eveline's room, soothing my hair with fussy, trembling hands. Her lamp was lit still. underneath the door I saw its gleam and turned the knob. Naked she lay, one arm across her eyes. Her nipples glistened, quivered on their crests, were moist.

'Eveline?'

'Emily? Someone came and kissed me, took my nightdress off. And it was dark. I know not who it was', she said.

CHAPTER 2

'Did you sleep with Rose last night?', Mama asked after breakfast when our guests had gone.

'Rose?', I asked, 'Rose?'

'The girl whose things you went upstairs to see. Or did you not?'

'Oh yes—I did a little, yes. She fell asleep so quickly, though. I went back to my room at last'.

I blushed. I tried to hide my blush, but I could not.

'I have noticed in dreams an instantaneous transition from one state to another, from one action to another, that does not occur in our waking lives. Instantaneous', said Papa. He unfolded his newspaper as he spoke and held it up before him—gazed into its pages. As if I could see his eyes; as if I could see his eyes.

'Am I as slim, my skin as fair, as when you married me?', Mama asked him.

'Instantaneous. There is no sense of suspension between one moment and another', said Papa.

Was it in part an answer to her question? Such subtleties were often spoken in our house. I felt that he was wrong, yet dared not say so. At the moment of the utmost warmth and moisture in my honeypot the night before; at the moment of the electric tingling of another's tongue within my mouth, all had seemed instantaneous. All moments merged into the next.

Mama was jealous, perhaps, of Adelaide. I felt a spite for her myself. Had she put her tongue in Papa's mouth last night? In his solidity, his breadth, his strength, solemn of demeanour as he often was, I thought it quite impossible. And yet her corsage had been loosed and half her breasts exposed in seeming readiness. And Eveline, her nightgown off and nipples risen. Quite plump already were her yearling tits. Many such have I since caressed and known the ineluctable, firm-silky feel of them. Their very brazenness invites the palm to shape the waiting globes.

Eveline and James had gone to play, Mama said. Often she said 'play', though we three were too old for such.

I found them in the narrow walk between the conservatory and the potting shed. Eveline was struggling closely in James' arms. Her hand was down between them and I saw his cock, the helmet ruby and the stem brown-white.

I stayed my steps. They had not seen me then.—'Don't! Stop it, no!', said Eveline. James' neck was flushed; he held her dress half up, her stockings white around her slim, young legs.

'Hold it, you silly'.—'No, won't! Oh!'

Her dress up at the back, her drawers tight-filled. He palmed the close-sheathed cheeks and felt beneath. I had my mouth go dry; my face felt hot.

'What do you do?', I asked, and Eveline sprang back. I saw her garters, pale flash of her thighs.

'I did not mean to; it was James' fault', she said and made to tug her dress down, but I stepped before her and I seized her wrist. James grinned at me, his trousers all agape and stalk up-sticking to my view. So fresh, so firm it looked, I felt a thrill of sin in me.

'I shall tell Mama', said Eveline and tried to tug away. James said, 'She is a sillikins; she won't'.

'Best not to say, best not to speak', said I. A slur of footsteps sounded and a maid approached, dustpan in hand, to empty it perhaps. She had not seen us. Round the corner, rushing, bumping, giggling of a sudden ran we three, James with his naughty thing still sticking out. He leaned against the sunburned wall and grinned at us with that unease that males have when they are in lust.

'It's naughty', Eveline said, but she still stared at it.

'You were naughty last night, were you not?', I asked, and of a sudden pushed her to him, bright with newfound excitement as I felt.

James clasped her, belly to his cock. She squealed.

'Oh, shush!', I said, and then the maid came round the corner, came on us, and stood stock-still, she stood and stared. Her arms limp, legs apart, she stared, the dustpan dangling from one hand. Fine cloud of dust like fairies in the light.

'Mary, come here', I said to her. I felt a tautness, in me, an excitement tight, like a constriction in my throat. My sister turned her face away, cried out. Her hips turned, and the maid saw James' cock.

'Miss, I got work to do'.

She looked as we had looked and saw it clear, its urgency upthrusting from his balls.

I set my teeth. I had a wild foolishness upon me then, perhaps. Eveline leaned back from James and caught the mood of me and said, 'Yes, Mary, do. Emily will give you half a sovereign if you do'.

'No, Miss, I . . .'

'Mary, come HERE! A sovereign it will be, I promise you. Come—touch it, feel it nice and firm', I said.

'No, Miss, please, Miss . . .'. But Eveline leapt, gazelle-like did she leap, her face in flush as was my own and grabbed at Mary's wrist and drew her close. The dustpan clattered down. Its tinplate quivered on the flagstones, then was still.

'I can't!' The maid's teeth chattered, but we had her close and pressed the blackness of her skirt to James who clasped her waist and boldly kissed her neck. Her hands were clenched. I forced her fingers open, though, in spite of it, and put them to his prick and whispered,

'Yes, a sovereign, Mary—a whole sovereign', in her ear.

'Ah, no, it's wicked, Miss—don't make me do!' She struggled, twisted, writhed within his clasp while Eveline drew the maid's skirt up and laughed. She had nice legs and was no more than seventeen or so. Her calves were slender and her thighs were plump, fresh as a turkey's, plump and white.

'She has no drawers on', James said. Both his hands had shifted from her waist—were up her skirt. The maid's arms strained against him and her head hung back. My sister seized her hair and pulled it down to make her neck strain back the more. White of her throat, her lips apart. She moaned but did not squeal out loud. James rolled her skirt up to her hips. Beside them—leaning close against—I saw his pego poking underneath her dell.

'No sir! No, Miss! Oh, please! Ah—OOOH!'

They were too close, too close for me to see, and curiously I felt a fear for her at that stiff poker underneath her quim.

'No, James—wait! Put it in her mouth instead!'

I knew not why I said it, with my head a-spin. The maid was sobbing, yet there were no tears.

'Oho, yes, inbetween her lips!', said Eveline and clasped the maid's slim waist and made her bend, as I did too, my hand upon her head until the swollen crest was at her mouth and dong-like brushed against her rosy lips.

'Ho...ho...ho...hold her nose', James gritted, and I felt for it and did. She snorted, wriggled, but then finally sucked breath in through her mouth and, with it open, in his knob was slid. I saw the inches, pinky-white, absorbed. 'T...t...two sovereigns!', stuttered James and I said 'Yes!' and saw saliva on his stalk that then was half-embedded in her mouth while Eveline had bared the girl's round bottom and was feeling it.

14

I watched James' face. His mouth went slack. *I want to see her eyes*, the man had said of me and I, remembering, took note of James' slack look, the presence of a wonderment, a charm.

'Oooh-wer, I'm feeling her!', said Evelyn and laughed.

'T . . . t . . . two sovereigns if she sucks', said James again.

The maid was snorting less. I loosed my fingers from her nose and heard her slurping as she drew upon the piston of his hot desire, hips wriggling to my sister's fingers underneath her bottom where the sunlight gleamed on her twin orbs.

'Oh, darling!' Gasping, suddenly my mouth was close to James', and one hand lightly placed on Mary's head. Mouth then to mouth we kissed. Warm, hurried breathings and wet tongues a-touch.

'Goo-goo-goo-goooh!', he gurgled and I felt his hips a-shake. A glubbing sound came from the maid's own mouth. James' eyes screwed up; he sucked upon my tongue. 'Dooo-doo-doo-doooh!', he stammered on my tongue. I knew him to be wetting—coming—then. His form was all a-shake, a-shake throughout. The maid was spluttering. James' breath hissed fiercely to my own—legs shook—and then he drew his dripping penis out.

'SPMMMF!', Mary spluttered. Skirt up still, we let her rise, hand to her mouth and wiping it.

'Oh! I am going in!', said Eveline in a panic then, and ran. Her footsteps sounded far, then she was gone. James grinned the weakest grin; his cock hung limp, was smeared around the knob and rosier than when he had first put it in.

'OH-WOH!', the maid sobbed.— 'There, there, shush', said I. I put my arms around her and James slid away. He buttoned up his trousers as he went. I rather hated him for his cowardice, and thought all males were so, perhaps. After they had come, as it was called.

'I didn't, didn't want to!', Mary sobbed, though still there were no tears. I soothed her hair. We clung as skylarks cling in summer to a wall.

'You will have your money, honestly', I said.

'Don't want it, don't!' She wiped her lips again. I wondered at the volume he had spilled within, and knew her cry to be a false one by the tone of it.

'Come, Mary, don't be silly; yes, you do. Come to my room now—come indoors. Oh, what a jape it was', I laughed. My laugh was tinsel, though. I had a warmth between my thighs and sensed that she too had.

'I shall be told off now', she snivelled as we walked away.

'You shall not be, Mary. I will say, if asked, that my dress was snagged against the hedge and that you helped me get it free. Tompkins will dare say naught to me', I said, referring to the housekeeper we then had.

'You don't have to give me anyfink', she whined. I wished her not to whine—wished her to walk upright, lips parted at the wonder of it as I thought I would myself have done.

Mama was in the morning room and saw us enter, scolded Mary for her wrinkled dress, but I—explaining in a mumble that we had fallen down—took the girl upstairs and to my room. She stood there humbly while I closed the door, sought for my purse and handed her a coin. She would not take it till I pressed it to her palm.

'Master James will give you another, Mary; I will see to it'.

'Don't want it, Miss'. But even so, she clasped her hand around the shining piece.

'It is not for *earning*, Mary. Do not think of it as such, but for a pleasure spent, and yet another you may spend upon your own. Did it taste funny, nice? Oh tell me, do'.

'Dunno, Miss'. There was crimson in her cheeks. I sensed in her that girlish urge I often had myself to laugh and cry in the same moment.

'It was not horrid, really? Was it? No?'

'It tasted funny .... well, not nasty, no. It's .... '

'Go on, Mary, tell me, do. I often wanted ... well ... to do the same'.

'Tastes creamy, salty. There was ever such a lot!' She giggled suddenly, then choked and held her hand up to her mouth. She smiled, she bit her lower lip. I could not help but do the same and hugged her to me. Stiff at first, she then relented, let me hold her close. I felt her belly warm to mine, her thighs.

'I will get the other sovereign for you, Mary—give it you tonight'.

'All right, Miss, yes. I'll get a bonnet, a new dress, and hide the rest away, I will'.

'I bet it throbbed! Oh, Mary, did it throb?'

Her eyes were bright, her lips were close to mine. I wanted much to kiss her, but instead I soothed her cheeks. Her breath was milky, pleasant, with a scent of sperm such as I had known upon the bed. She did not answer, dropped her eyes. Our noses touched and tickled. Hard her breasts felt up against my own.

'Would you do it again, Mary, if I asked you to?'

'Dunno, Miss'.

'*Would* you, Mary?'

'Might. I shouldn't, though—should I? You said. ... Oh, Miss, you said...'

'I said I'd thought of it. I have. I haven't done it, though, myself. I will do, though, I know I will. But not with Master James, of course. *There*—now we have a secret each. I will not tell, and nor will you'.

'Oh no, I never would, Miss, no. I darst not. They would turn me out. My Dad would be that angry with

me that I don't know what. I never done it that way,
Miss, before'.

'But you *have* done it, though? Oh, tell me. . . .
No, not now perhaps, or Mama will wonder at your
absence and our solitude'.

'Yes. Better go, Miss'.

Startled at our boldness, she released herself, ran
out. I leaned against the door as Eveline did. I had
kissed James upon the mouth—had put my tongue
between his lips. His cock had jetted into Mary's while
we did. My head a-spin, my quim a-throb, I eased my
dress up, felt my bottom warm against the moulding
of the door and touched my lovelips through the cot-
ton's veil. Head buzzing, eyelids drooping, I began to
rub, but then was startled into otherness.

A loud knock sounded. Papa called my name.

CHAPTER 3

'It is Arnold', said Papa. I felt
dismayed and disarrayed.

'Oh? Why then did not the maid come?', asked I
and felt a thrill of wonderment and apprehension cours-
ing through my veins at my impertinence.

'Mary is not to be found, the valet has injured his
leg, and. . . . Why do you ask?'

'I beg your pardon, Papa; I did not think'.

I felt a guilt at what had passed and also had a sense
of irritation to be disturbed at such a moment, dress
up and my calves on view.

'Indeed? Have you a fever? You appear to me quite
flushed'.

His look absorbed me, and I had the strangest feeling that I saw him and yet saw him not. His eyes became
transparent. Through them I could see again the merriment outside, against the wall, and wondered if it,
too, were in his head, in my strange fancy, though he
could not know.

'I was playing, father, and I just came up'.

'You are beyond such sport now, are you not? Your
activities henceforth should be otherwise. Give thought
to it, my dear, for Arnold has a serious intent—I do
believe he has. Indeed, he has spoken of intentions,
privately to me, of which I find approval. Are you of
the same mind—to wed?'

I turned my back on him. Dismay showed in my
eyes. Arnold was four years older than myself. His father
was a merchant, though so rich that Society forgave
him that. His mother was a little vulgar, so I thought—
his sisters strange.

'Papa, he has not. . . .'

'Not what?' Approaching me as he then did, I hunched my shoulders and I blushed. It seemed an oddity to say what I then needed to. Mama I might have said it to, but not Papa.

'He has not even kissed me yet'.

So tightly and with such embarrassment the words came that my throat was as a tube from which one squeezes water, urging out the drops.

'Not kissed, not kissed? Such is not to be taken as a token or a promise. Many people kiss whose thoughts are at the same time of another—hence there then is little value to it, or they may have but a passing fancy for the moment, upon which—having savoured the lips they sought—they find the least fulfilment therein. Arnold will inherit much. The only son, you know'.

'I know that, yes, Papa'.

I did not turn, I would not turn. I hated what he said, or had no liking for it at the least.

'I am to be sold, then? Am I to be sold?'

My bitterness surprised me, yet I could not help but say. James had leaned against the wall. The maid had succoured, sucked, him. There was freedom there. Against the wall, against the sunlit wall. Mary would not be immured in marriage just for that.

'It is the way of things that women are given in marriage, Emily'.

'Is it?' My ire was up, and such as I had never known before. I, meek in Papa's presence always, was a rebel now. I had my cause. The swallows flew against the tall blue sky all summer long and never landed. Never had I seen one need to rest upon a bough. I wished, I wished, to be as them—to fly, to fly.

'I have often kissed you, Emily. 'Tis but a token— not a promise never to be broken'.

His voice was softer. I did not receive the strictures, reprimand, I had expected. Face to face we stood, I turning, twirled, by guiding hands and brought to face, nose tickled by his black cravat, my hair a little rumpled and no powder on my cheeks.

'It is not the same', I mumbled, knowing not how I should put my arms, my hands. I let them fall, held them against my skirt.

'You must be guided by your elders, Emily. Mark this kiss—it shall be no more, no less, than others are'.

So saying, he lifted up my chin. Uncomprehending (I could not do otherwise) I allowed his lips to fall, full fall, upon my own, O lightly at the first but then they pressed, merged, moistened, mouths became as one mouth yet were two. I felt a dizziness and clutched his arms. His chest absorbed the firmly jellied pressure of my breasts. My shoulders were enfolded—the whole length of my slim body pressed to his; his thighs were tree-trunks to my own. Hands shaped my back and pondered at my bottom's bulb, tasting the twin globes that they found beneath my dress.

One minute, two perhaps, we breathed, thus breathed, upon each other's tongue, and there was wilderness and wildness in my mind, a hollow sounding as of songs I never heard before. Weak were my knees, my bottom plumlike poised upon his palms.

'In such a moment . . .' Thickly did he speak, lips parting slowly from my own, and turned away, hands trembling faintly on the windowsill, I felt as a lone tree where once a forest stood. 'You should brush your hair', he said, his back to me. Awkwardly moving then, he turned towards my door, touched at the handle and then hesitated, I feeling as one who had somehow vaguely sinned, and he the victim.

'Brush my hair, Papa, yes'.

If I continued to look at him he would not leave, I thought, and knew not why I thought. In such small fragments of time it is as if something tangible, a cord, a chain, secures both speakers and is stretched almost to tautness, but not quite.

'And you will speak with Arnold, speak with him?'

'If you so wish, Papa, I shall'.

The words, for no reason I could think of, brought a sigh from him. *If I were naked now,* I wished to say, madness possessing me—the bizarre turn that my mind had often taken since my greater youth. Do the thoughts of all turn in such labyrinths where dreams and devils lurk, competing, each with tickets in their hands for entertainments one should never see?

'I wish. . . .'

He spoke, he sighed again, was gone, the impress of my bottom on his palms, the weight still tingling on his fingertips. Yet if I thought *that*. . . . Did I think it then, or was the moment like to an old dress that one discovers and recovers, furbishes anew with other buttons, other ribbons, lace replaced?

Arnold awaited me—the tall, the spare. I had seen James' stiff prick and thought of Arnold's as a thin and withered one, a stalk that drooped and never showed its pride, his testicles all shrunken underneath. Fear of the sun, the open light.

Nor was I the only one who thought such thoughts. That evening, long after Arnold had departed, Mama asked me what he said.

'He said to marry me', I said. When there is bitterness, one spares one's words. Some women spill them out, but I do not.

'Is he equipped?' asked Jane. Covering up her mouth she spoke, and laughed.

'It is not needful so to ask', Mama replied.

I looked beyond them through the window where the sun in its slow falling rendered up a last illumination to an elm. I felt its bark, its roughness, from a distance—felt the long, slow, soft-slow flow of sap, felt it within.

22

'When I marry Arnold, if I do, then you may see it, too', said I.

'Oh, really, do not speak so', Mama said and left the room. Her skirts swoosh-swished in walking as she walked.

'Even so, she will listen at the door', said Jane, and whispered, 'May I see Arnold's really, if you do?'

'You may, you might. I have not seen it yet. Mama told me that such jollities may be contained if one knows how to go about it, is discreet. I have seen a penis in its rising, seen. Have you?'

'In the dark corners of the house and by the wells of stairs at dusk, I have'.

'Whose, then? Oh, tell me whose?'

'Whose did *you* see?'

'Oh-ho, can't tell you—honestly, I daren't. You are extremely naughty sometimes, Jane'.

'I know. But when one's thighs are felt, the urge to touch in turn is quite intrinsic, is it not? I love to have my bottom held and soothed. Do you?'

'Sometimes when I am kissed I do. But never has my dress been drawn up yet, has yours?'

She knew my story-telling for the blush upon my cheeks and touched them, felt them warm and kissed my nose, tip of my nose she kissed and then my brow.

'Once in the stable, Emily, and only once, my drawers broke and they fell, fell to my ankles like a fallen crown, mouth open and my face aflame. He felt me, felt between my thighs, skirt heavy, looped across his arm. Mama said we might take domestic pleasures as we find them, did she not? The male must be the master totally, or else must be a pet to be handled just as we. She said that, said'.

'I know. The thought is absolutely awesome, is it not? Yet desperately exciting. Who was in the stable with you? Who?'

'Do you not know? Is innocence your veil'? Mama

asked. 'If you have been mastered, Jane, then speak not of it. In your womanhood surrender as you must, your legs apart. When one is woken, stirred from early sleep, hips upward turned, the bedclothes all cast down and nightgown raised, hand clamped around one's mouth, how can one squeal or dare to try? He nests his cock in me and holds it in, his balls tight up to me until I'm still. And then he pumps me as I wriggle, breathing hot upon his palm. The first time—oh!—my eyes were wild as starlings at the first shots of the guns in the far fields beyond, beyond'.

'You let him do it to you now?'

Our tongue tips touched. Hands fluttered, sought uncertainly, then fell.

'He smacks my legs to keep them open sometimes—does'.

'Oh, is it . . . ? Tell me who! Oh, tell me do. You can do it with Arnold if I marry him. I shall, I think. I *came* this afternoon, I almost did!'

'Often enough you will. O treasured bliss it is! Play with yourself tonight and think of it. At dinner parties here—I was abed the last time, but I know. . . .'

'Know what?' Mama had entered, cast her gaze on us, and in particular on me.

'How nice your dinner parties are, Mama', I interjected quickly, and Jane squeezed my hand, said it was true, and then herself went out.

'Do not tell her too much', Mama said. She caused me then to blush and fiddle with my gown. 'Those who are too loose with their tongues lose self-possession, Emily. Bear that in mind always. What date have you then fixed?'

'I have not, Mama'.

'Do it soon, my love. Many are the preparations that we have to make. September is a good month, is it not?'

'Yes, Mama'.

24

I was close to tears, although she knew it not. The long night on the bed upstairs seemed long gone then. I wanted once again a tongue between my thighs.

Upon retiring, Papa met me on the stairs and escorted me along the corridor.

'It is September, then', he said—had clearly listened, or Mama had told him so.

'September, yes'. The sad song of the year. Dying of leaves and winds that wait on the horizon's rim. A dolefulness was on me and I wished again to cry. My room received me as rooms do receive—the furniture that waits to speak and yet cannot, most stolid of all servants that one knows. Wanting to throw myself upon the carpet, plead with it to bear my footsteps still, and ever on.

He closed my door and leaned against it. Eveline would lean to hers and hear me if I did not whisper in the night.

'When you kiss, Emily, keep your lips apart'.

Mama said legs, had said to Jane so, but I said it only in my head and kept a deep, soft blankness in my eyes.

'Yes, Papa'.

'If I show you—were to show'.

The room was frozen, and the furniture was blind.

'I . . . I will keep my lips apart, Papa. A little, just a little, yes'.

'Yes . . . ah . . . Goodnight, then, Emily, goodnight.'

'Goodnight, Papa.'

My drawers off, playing with myself, when he had gone, had gone. I heard—I thought I heard—a cry, faint cry, from Jane's room and a squeaking, bumping of her bed. And then I slept, I slept, I slept.

CHAPTER 4

I was to be given away much
as is a piece of furniture that
has known its better days in other houses, other rooms—
to be transported to another territory, put to crochet
work, tea parties and receptions, put upon display.

'It is true, my pet, but do not cut your arguments
with a blunt knife', Mama said when I uttered up my
thoughts to her. 'She who swims with the current, Emily,
can often find a better shore, a secret cove or two, a
mite of sunlight others have not glimpsed. Be thus and
thus as is a sapling under snow. The snow melts and
it springs upright again, no worse for the weight and
cold opinions of the burden that it bore. When you are
being naughty, though, indulge yourself with all discretion and with quietness such as will not disturb those
whom you do not wish to know of it'.

'You must have a stable, then', said Jane, and
laughed. She had rolled her bottom several times in
ours—had come flush-faced and told me almost all.

'You may both be tested still. Make not a mockery
of it', Mama said, and then—regarding me carefully
and with such a look as bids one not to respond directly
to what is said—she added, 'You, Emily, are our first
to wed. There will be jollities—be sure of that'.

'Yes, Mama', I said, while Jane clapped her hands
and remarked, 'Oh, you will be *sportif*, then?'

'Shush', Mama said, 'she may be as she will. Mo-
desties may have to be abandoned on the day; I see no
help for it'.

'It means our drawers may droop', said Jane afterwards to me. I gazed at her askance. 'You know well

what I mean', she added, and gave me a tender and appraisive look.

'No, I do not', I answered, for her clever ways had cause to irritate me sometimes, but at that she raised her eyebrows and cocked her head.

'The *droit de seigneur*? You have not heard of it? He who chooses to be your Master on or just before your wedding day has the first rights to you. Your husband cannot say him nay'.

'Oh, I do not believe that, Jane', I said with pettishness, but as the days and weeks went by I had a sense of an encumbrance on my being, a sense of waiting; eyes appraised me as they never had before. My legs, I felt, were seen beneath my skirt, and the protuberance of my breasts, my bottom, measured, just as I was measured for a wedding gown. Beneath its frills, its taffeta and lace, I was to wear a waist corset and a camisole of silk. Drawers were not mentioned.

'As to drawers, Mama', I said, but before I could complete the sentence, she had interrupted me.

'On such a day you do not cover up too much, my love. The reception will be private, after all. There are tastings to be considered. Be obedient and you may yet surpass us all. The men must have their merriments— the ladies, too', came her reply. And I, seeking in my sudden maze of thoughts no explanations from her, turned to my cousin, Julie, who had come to stay with us.

'Tastings? What did she mean?', I asked. Julie was of my own age, height and figure, svelte of hips. She often had a sly look in her eyes. We lay abed, our nightgowns rucked up to our thighs.

'Oh, Emily, you do not know? I was tasted on my eighteenth birthday; sometimes it is done. You must display your pussy first—not look too shy nor look too eager. *Tasting* only means the lightest touch, above, below, and yet it makes one quiver so. I knew not where

28

to put my eyes, holding my skirts up as I did, was bid to. First, the gentlemen all touched my bottom, then my cunnylips, oh lightly, lightly, but it tickled so. The ladies bent and passed their tongues up inbetween my thighs. I felt the flickering of wet tips there and jerked my bottom, but was smacked and told to stand, to stand upright, knees straight and legs apart. Then I was taught to kiss. Have you been taught?'

'A little, yes'. I blushed within the dark.

'Touchings of tongues, your lips apart, and titties, bottom, felt? I felt my knees weaken. Full a dozen tongues came in my mouth. Each cupped my thing— my cunny, quim. I, swoony, swaying, clipped my thighs, but they were slapped apart again. It does not matter who it is who kisses you or feels your fur, soothes fingers underneath your belly or explores your bottom's curves. Some ladies, licking me, said I was creamy there'.

'Oh, Julie, are you?' Head swirling with her wicked words, I upped her nightgown and exposed her curls, she wriggling, giggling, lying back, extending her warm thighs apart. Her thatch was dark and wondrous, and the lips beneath were tinged with pink and moist as a cut peach.

'Don't do it—no, you mustn't, Emily....' But even as she spoke she pressed my head down, down, lips slipping on the soft, silk skin, whorl of her belly button and a musky scent, aroma of the female who is coming up on heat. 'Goo-goo!', she choked, for I had found her curls beneath my mouth and then—with tracing tongue—her spot, whimper of acorn flesh that quivered, rose, and like a tiny penis came erect.

Shifting I shifted, wriggling further down, toes snarling in the wrinkled sheet until my face came up between her thighs. 'Taste me!', she moaned and pressed her bottom down bringing my nose up just above her mount, inviting me to search her with my tongue. Her cunnylips were puffy, pouting out. I toiled my tongue between the shell-like folds and found again her waiting clitoris, bringing a squeal of joy from her.

'Like this?' My voice came hollow from the deep, dark deep, between the ruffled sheets. Her heels dug in, her bottom jerked.

'Oh yes, oh yes, oh yes, oh yes', she moaned, slip-slobbery my mouth against her quim, the salt of her, the musky-warm aroma of our kind, gliding my palms beneath her roguish bottom cheeks to hold their wriggling still while I licked on. Words burst inside my head like starshells, but I could not speak. I heard her grimace her pleasure to the dark, dark of my darkling room, and then she spilled, salt-savour of her seepings on my tongue that rapidly was coated with her cream.

'Oh, Emily! Oh yes, oh yes! Again!'

I wanted all, though, all, and worked my body up, my nightgown wreathing up above my breasts and found hers bare and brought them tip to tip, brush of my muff to hers—brush-tingling of our swollen titties then. She poised them, made them roll together, tip to tip, raising her legs criss-crossed around my waist. Dance of our hips and spillings from our cunnies and our tongues, we threshing, incoherent, mouth to mouth. And in...

... And in the quiet that followed, in the quiet, came such caressings as can make the lustiest of males seem bores at times—which is to say, when they have threaded one and lie cock-limp, oftimes begin to snore, the globbings from their reservoirs all done.

In Sapphic pleasures all is otherwise. 'Tis delicate, long-laboured often, and is sweet. One lies in pure contentment, arms relaxed, thighs sprawled apart and fingers intertwined with murmurations of a fond desire which has a selflessness most males eschew, or know not how to bring to it.

'Tasting is nice', said Julie, and I said 'Yes', —said 'Yes', I said, in some naivete as we both were. I had longed learned to kiss—I knew it then—but with a male it was an otherness. Yet even so the creeping vines of warm desire were intertwining in my veins. Julie's head drooped on my shoulder and she slept while I meandered in the rose arbours of my thoughts. There were dreams to be had here; I, and that old lady of the past, had both been right.

'What happened afterwards—after your tastings?', I wished to ask of Julie, but her breath was soundless in her slumbering, or seemingly she slept, but as a gentle knock came on my door and I heard the slightly squeaking handle turn, I lay back with my eyes closed while at the same time I felt my cousin stir. The door opened, creaked, and then was stilled. Footfalls upon the carpet, and I turned my back, presenting shoulders only to the visitor.

Papa! I knew it by his breathing then. 'Julie', he murmured softly. She sat up. I felt her bottom shifting up the sheet, and hoped her nightgown to be fully down.

'I have not heard you say your prayers, as I was asked to do', he said.

'I'm sorry—I forgot'. A whispered squeak, and I affected then a little snore.

'Come, do it now, but let us both be quiet. You do not need your wrap. Come now'.

'Yes'. Hushed and timid was her tone. Her legs swung out of bed, the bedclothes dragged, dragged down, revealed my bottom where my robe was up. I did not move but hunched my shoulders tight, and she retreating, bare feet on the floor. A mumbling from without, and they were gone, along the corridor, the deep warm sleekness of the silent night. I heard the study door click open quietly, heard the whisper-slither of her toes upon the carpet there within.

Whenever people mumble in the night, I think of goblins, small and fat, with mouths that never part beyond an inch. I think of gloomy furniture that never sleeps, inky shadows, of deserted stairs that wait upon the first feet on the morn, the maids' thighs twinkling underneath their skirts, hot tea upon their lips, the kitchen cold and vaster than it looks when day has spread its light more fully.

Soft mumblings, yes, I heard. A little 'Oh!' from Julie, then a bump, a thump, as though a pot had fallen on a cushion, such a sound was made.

My floorboards creaked. I wished they did not creak, yet knew by sense and sensing where they bent and, slipping from the bed, tiptoed as if on numbered squares to reach my door. It had been left ajar. I opened it, heart-thumping, heard a small, quick 'GLOOO!' from Julie, and then quiet again, or almost quiet, save for the tiny sounds that filter through the walls at night, the ghosts of bats, of leaves that died and seek the tree whence they long were blown.

Forward I sneaked, and knew my every edging tread.

'A little more', I heard Papa say, stilled myself, then ventured on again in such fell gloom as makes a yard seem as a furlong is. His door was open and I saw a light within. No sound of prayers came, but another sound, a lipping, squishy-soft sound and a hissing as from Julie's nose.

Oh, venture on, my heart said, but I did not dare. For one long moment just the door absorbed me, and the bar of light. Then—AH!—a hand clamped from behind across my mouth. An arm encompassed my small waist. The voice of Jane was a fluff-ball in my ear.

'Be quiet, be quiet, you may just for a moment look', she said.

I made to kick. I dared not kick nor move, so tense was my astonishment and, overall, the great fear that Papa might know me there or hear her voice and come out to confront us both.

32

'Now move. . . .', I heard and inch by inch we neared
the door, my bottom bulbing to her belly as we moved—
a dance, slow dance, of terrified enchantment. Closer
and closer came the light, and then I saw within, eyes
bulging and her hand still at my mouth.

Papa sat foursquare on a simple wooden chair, his
legs apart, his trousers ruffled down, though all that I
could see were trunklike thighs, the back of Julie's head.
She knelt between his legs, her head was bent. One
hand was forward and the other somewhere underneath. Her head bobbed and I heard a slurping sound.
Papa half closed his eyes and murmured to himself,
his hands gripped on the raised arms of the chair. Squishy
the sounds, as I had heard before, and then I was half-
drawn, half-lifted back, propelled around and guided
down the stairs.

I sniffled, burbled, but dared make no noise. The
stairs creaked and crackled like emergent flames. Not
until the drawing room was reached did Jane release
my mouth.

'What? Oh!' —I knew not what to say.

'A brandy—shall we steal one each?', she laughed.

'What?', I repeated, feeling rather like a parrot who
has learned just that. I made to sit, in my bewilderment,
but started up again. More footfalls slithered and Mama
came in, floating her fine form in a nightgown of blue
silk. The world was upside down—I knew it to be so.
She must have passed the study door, the bar of light
and Julie there and . . .

'A half a glass and that is all', she said, picked up
a cushion, placed it down again and gazed at me appraisingly as Jane procured a carafe, glasses, and a tray.

'Mama. . . .', I bleated, but Jane shook her head.

'Sometimes I want to cry, sometimes to laugh. Are
we not all so?', Mama asked. The lamps that Jane had
lit shone through her nightgown, and she wore no
drawers. All liquid were our movements. 'The three

Graces', said Mama and took her glass, we standing as might people in a park who stop to speak and then pass on. She tilted back her head, emptied her glass and bid me do the same. I did so, choked a little and then coughed.

'Discretion is the first thing that we learn—is that not so, Mama?', Jane asked. She slid her free arm round my waist and soothed my bottom gently as she spoke.

'The wedding will be a fine one', said Mama. She spun her glass between her fingers. The rim sparkled, then she drained the final drop. Her tongue peeped pinkly, then withdrew. 'How gently goes the night when all is done and well done, and with quietude, my pets. You have both learned to kiss and stir your hips a little; that is good. Julie will return to you in but a moment, Emily. Go back to bed now'.

'Yes, Mama'.

'She will cuddle you, I do expect', Jane said, but then was shushed. I watched her pick the carafe up. The brandy swilled within the fine, glass globe. I hesitated. Mama pouted at me, said, 'Go on, my pet', and forwarded her glass then up to Jane once more to let the heady liquid spill within.

I wandered lonely as a cloud, as Mr. Wordsworth says. The stairs, dark stairs, received and swallowed me. A scuffling sounded up above; the study door was closed and then on entering my room again I found my cousin back upon my bed, hands up behind her head, her legs apart, lace of her nightgown round her belly's curve, and her dark bush displayed.

'Emily—come and kiss me.' She extended one arm and then tucked it back.

'No', I said, 'No'.

'You have to come to bed'. Smile in the dark—a cat's smile and I hated her.

'There are times when you have to, Emily, and this is one of them'. The voice was not hers, though, but

34

Mama's, who had followed me so quietly that I knew not she was there.

'Mama—she...' Oh, I almost said the words!

'She *what*? Get into bed, my love. Receive the night, receive the night'.

The door was closed. I stumbled forward, all a-maze, head dizzy, and a tingling in my nest I wished there not to be, but Julie's arms enfolded me and drew me down. Her open legs received mine, though I fretted, struggled, then for fear of more alarms, excursions, I lay still and let my belly palpitate on hers.

'Emily, you are a sillikins sometimes. Come—put your tongue into my mouth', she urged.

I spluttered softly, would not do. Her pussy rubbed to mine, her legs hooked mine and held them wide apart. My nightgown raised, our tits were bare again.

'Tasting is nice', said Julie and she stung my tongue, a bee's sting with her own, made my head swim.

'Noo, nooo!' I mumbled, but her legs spread more, rose up, calves crossed in ringlike strength around my waist.

'Rock your bottom, Emily. Oh, nice it is!'

'I shan't!'

'You shall!'

'Oh, stop it, do, you hateful, wicked... oooh!' Mouths open warm and I surrendering, the oily lips of passion there below, between our legs, writhing against each other's as we squirmed.

'You don't know what I did', she mouthed, fur of her bush a-tickling under mine.

'I do. You... OOOF!' Her finger at my bottom-hole. It entered and I squealed into her mouth, tried to resist it, but it wormed within and held me pinned upon her lambent warmth, our nipples rubbery and stiff.

'Come on, come on!', she puffed.

'Don't w... w... want to....'

There was a saltiness upon her tongue. Her lips were rimed with drying cream.

The scent of sperm. I knew it for its savour and its headiness, alike to chestnut blossom, as I thought it then.

'I said my prayers', she laughed beneath my mouth. Far gone, too gone to fret rebellion then, I squirmed my hips, spilled out my spendings, trilling with her own, soared into white clouds tinged with pink and deeper promises of purple far beyond.

'His balls—they were my rosary', she said, and whirling like a leaf I fell, down, down, oh down, into the liquid bliss.

CHAPTER 5

'Many are the marriages made on the moon, and thence the greater part of them should go. Yours is not one of them—no freedom is denied you, nor shall be', Mama said to me on my wedding eve, endeavouring to toss such crumbs of comfort as she could, and yet not coddling me at all.

I was directed and diverted as a small stream is, its gullies, channels, passages rock-blocked, stone-hindered, and the glittering waters turned aside to find a new path through a meadow dark, unknown.

Therewith there grew in me a hardness that at first I did not recognise, though as a ball of wool is—tossed about a room—I gathered scraps of other colours to me, stardust that had sprinkled on the floor when humans were not there, and specks and flecks of satisfied desire that fell from under skirts of those more wanton than I then was. My imagination thus was in some rout, yet equally it gathered up a sense of things the more the hours passed to my wedding noon.

Upon the afternoon beforehand, when many were the voices in the house, James came to me as I sought solitude and begged me to accompany him to his room. He had been smoking—nervously, I thought—had the aroma of his jacket and looked flushed.

'Only a moment, then', said I. We entered and he closed the door. His room was in a disarray, his guns uncased, books opened everywhere, a pair of Norfolk britches on the bed.

'I would kiss you as I kissed you once—against the

wall. Remember that?' He clasped my waist and drew me closely to him, thighs to thighs.

'No', I said weakly, but a hint of some excitement flourished in my belly then.

'Brothers and fathers have the first right, it is said', said James.

'Do they?', I answered. Lips touched lips. I meant them not to, but they did. The sticky mouth of Mary and my cousin's salty tongue. Visions of nightfall: mother drinking brandy with a smile. 'What is the claim?', I asked. I teased; I should say teased—our tongue tips touched. My skirt was eased up slowly by his hands. Air warm, cool-warm around my calves, my knees, and of a sudden then it was scooped up, my bottom plump upon his palms.

I strained at him, yet could not bear to lose the moment we had once begun when Mary mouthed him, sucked upon his tool.

'The claim is here, my sweet, between your cheeks, and up between your thighs where your tight nest will learn to suck upon the cock. Oh, let me feel it—let me get my hand within!'

He sought to tug my drawers down, but I stayed his hand. Strong as he was, he had an awe of me. Our eyes fought; I succumbed, against my better will I did.

'Don't, darling'. Yet my voice became a whine. He shook my hand away and stole his own beneath the waistband of my drawers, sought deep, and cupped my pulsing quim upon his palm.

'There—does it not feel nice?', he husked.

'Mmmm . . . yes!' The mood was on me and I could not help. His finger eased apart the lips and found the waiting moisture, rosy bud. Knees weakening, I made him hold me up and ringed my arms around his neck.

'Oh, let me cream you, love, upon the bed'.

'No, James, you mustn't, not yet, no'. I said *not yet*, I said *not yet*. I breathed as Julie breathed that night at prayer, my tendrils of warm breath against his own, I circled my tongue lazily within his mouth and cared not for the morrow or the afterwards. My drawers drooped, fell and circled in a white loop round my ankles, laces white against brown shoes.

'Open your legs more, Emily'.

'I won't'. Slow, hungered stirring of our mouths, his hidden prick rockhard against my thigh. He sought my bottom, held the cheeks apart and held me thus, skirt looped upon his arms.

In the stable, Jane was, yes, I know she was, I know with whom she was, I know...

'How plump your bottom is and yet how small it feels a-throbbing on my palms!'

'Does it?' My eyes rolled up, my head hung back, his kisses on my neck, tip of his finger easing in into my rosehole. 'D...d...d...don't!', I whimpered, but he would not stop, began to work it back and forth, in-out, and fingered up my cunny with his other hand, I arcing back, knees sagging, mouth agape, the ceiling a white cloud above. Blindly I sought him, felt his prick, the cloth around it, made the buttons loose and dipped my hand within around his stave.

'I will c...come!', he stammered.

Such semblance of control as I possessed surprised me then. I squeezed his pulsing rod and brought it burning to my silky belly as we stood.

'You won't', said I. The door swung open then, we frozen in lewd attitude like a forbidden statue, and there stood Papa.

Such moments hang in Time as does a raindrop on the petal of a rose. The floor creaked and was quiet again. Papa loosed a button of his jacket, let the sides fall free.

'James will go to his sister's room and there remain'. The words were sombre and yet spoken with a quiet. My brother gurgled something and tore free, I left forlorn, my skirt high as a band is round a cake, my fallen drawers hallucinating sins I had not quite discovered then.

James sought to cover up his tool. He could not, for too stiff it was, and blushing like a schoolgirl he ran out.

'Your drawers are down, my dear. A little early yet for frolics, is it not? Your garters should be tighter than they are. See to it on the morrow that they band your thighs as closely as your dreams'.

'Papa? Yes, Papa'. I squeaked. I did not recognise my voice. His jacket was dark brown and ribbed with braid. A white silk handkerchief peeped like a rabbit from his pocket top. I had to bend, to bend down for my drawers, but could not move—I, striken with dismay. My fingers opened, closed again, arms limp.

'Come here!'

'M . . . m . . . my drawers, Papa—I cannot move'.

'Come here, I say! Walk slowly and you will not fall. How like a stricken schoolgirl you do look. And yet . . .'

I blundered, almost tripped, and toed my way with wariness, though tried to hide such look as may have been upon my face. Ticklings of tinglings round my pussy, and my thighs were warm. Within a foot of him I stopped, I teetered, held myself upright, blushed full and tried to meet his gaze.

'That blush may be the last, my pet. I trust it may, except when you feel wrath or anger at some unkind thing. Adjust your stockings—have them ever tight'.

I bent, head at his stomach almost, finger-fretted, pulled, arranged, glimpsed a protuberance beneath my eyes, and straightened, almost falling sideways at the tugging of my drawers that were more tightly wreathed about my ankles, then.

'You have learned to kiss, I see—have learned to part your legs, if somewhat gauche your attitude. Your

knees will learn to tremble not, your body will be upright to a lingering touch. Be sharp upon your toes in
attitudes of passion, Emily. Spare not your poses, keep
your bottom thrust'.

'P . . . P . . . Papa?'

'Step back a pace and pull your drawers up, then
stand still'.

'Yes'. I—the submissive one who hated so to be—
obeyed and soothed my dress, my belly pale a longer
moment to his eyes as I arranged myself—fluff of my
bush. . . . His trouser-bulge was blatant, undismayed by
a quick skittering of eyes, my eyes.

'Autumn will be upon us soon—cries of the corn-
crakes, and the summer done'.

'Fires will be lit in all . . .' I stopped in my reply.
Hazed memories of three abed, a penis stirring lazy-
warm against my thigh.

'Indeed, my dear, in all the rooms, in all; I trust in
all. . . . That is to say . . .'

Awkwardly he moved, came to my side, penis pro-
truding upwards through his trousercloth, the poker
buried like a broken spear. It touched my knuckles—
hesitated—lingered with the quick self-consciousness
of an uncertain comma in a sentence. I moved my
hand a little, felt it stir, unwilting ramrod to my fingers
pressed.

'Yes, Emily yes', Papa said.

Was it a command? I hung my head, but let my
hand still touch. His loins stirred, and I felt the fuller
length brush right across the limp back of my hand. I
swallowed, and he heard the sound.

'I shall. . . .', I said. I knew not what to say. My
head was separated from my heart.

'Go to your room again? Indeed. Be watchful on
the morrow; do not take that which you do not need,
do not desire'.

'No, Papa'.

I slouched, moved forward to the door. I wished to flee, yet not to go, he standing motionless, his back to me. I should have been forlorn, yet felt not so. The good, the bad, the needed, the desired, became as one, were enveloped in silence, neither held or dropped.

James waited for me, sitting on my bed, face pale, his trousers buttoned up.

'What is to do—what is to do?', he asked, and stood confronting me.

'Naught that may bring dismay. Papa was kind. An understanding of the future bride', I sparkled, and surprised myself. 'He will not tell Mama, I know. Be sure of that'.

'Thank heavens for it. Did he...?'

'Did he what, James, what?'. A carelessness possessed me and I smoothed my hair.

'I mean, your drawers were down and...'

'Oh? Am I desirable?', I laughed. The ghost of Julie lingered on the bed. Her stockinged toes would tease their wicked tools, and they would humble stand like schoolboys, hands behind their backs.

'Extremely, Emily; you know you are. Such slim curves, yet such fullness. You would drive a statue to erect his prick'.

'I have done, I believe', I taunted him, then urged him to the door with playful touch. 'Go out, or Papa may return', I said. He wilted, bit his lip and went.

CHAPTER 6

After the incantations and the hymns—the promises we fractured as we spoke—bells, flowers, confetti, and the trailing of my long gown in the church, the world was born anew.

Arnold was quiet—looked like a soldier who had lost his gun, I thought. Returning home, I changed into a lighter garb laid out for me. The skirt, white taffeta with pink, was fluffed, had loose pleats and a ribbon hanging down. A blouse absorbed the fullness of my breasts. A large bow-tie I wore in the French fashion; it was modish then, had just come in. I wore white, patterned stockings with pink garters tight, but wore no drawers. I was at sacrifice.

'What an arse she has!', I heard on entering the drawing room where the private reception was arranged. Adelaide appeared and kissed my cheek, Pamela smiled, and her companion bowed. I had not seen them since that fateful night, but swore I would not blush, and did not do. Then Arnold's sisters were brought forward and arranged themselves to kiss me on both cheeks in turn.

'I will have your mouth tonight', the elder said. Her name was Constance; she was slim and tall. The other, Fiona, was quite small and neat, and a perky, lively air.

'You may or you may not', I said. I looked to Arnold, but his mother held his hand as though it were a glove she had long lost and now recovered. Father conversed with Adelaide and Mama stood with Jane and Eveline. Much punch was poured; a certain merriment obtained.

'Are you being querulous? You have not been tasted yet, and when you are...' So Constance murmured to me, but I cut her off.

I kept my smile. All hands had touched me in their passage, felt my bottom and caressed its cheeks. I had not jerked, I had not jerked at all. All eyes were bright around me and they watched my every movement—waiting, as I knew.

'I may employ an amanuensis', I replied. Unsure of the meaning of the word, I used it out of mischief.

'That is done?', she asked. She looked dismayed, and turned towards her father, Douglas, who stood bluff, undressed me with his eyes and then restored my blouse at least. I watched her speak to him and saw him nod. Papa held Adelaide close to his side, and I remembered how her breasts had shown. Upon a moment I was then confronted by my father-in-law. His lowered voice presaged a confidence he did not fully feel, I thought.

'It is done, my dear, but on the other hand there is a price to pay'.

'Indeed? My purse is empty', I replied.

All eyes were on me. I drank slowly from my glass, but did not take my eyes from his. He was not portly, nor was tall nor short. His waxed moustache was proud above his lip. An inner quivering I knew, but I stood still.

'Your lovenest will not be, my love. Not on this night nor any other, I believe. Forgive me for a moment', and—so saying—he stepped back across the room to speak to Papa and Mama. I stared at Adelaide. She blinked and smiled a smile uncertain, crossed her arms and then unfolded them. Jane winked at me. I emptied back my punch and felt my silk chemise against my quim—a curtain fluttering against my curls. I had a moisture of excitement there.

'It shall be Adelaide', I said, and all stood still. I

44

had interrupted, as it seemed, a conference of lewd intent.

'Yes, *Adelaide*!', laughed Jane, who caught my look.

'Not me! It is not fair!', squealed Adelaide and made to run. I barred the double doors to her. Papa came up and took her elbow in his hand.

'Stand still!', he barked at her. A servant entered unawares, stared at us and retreated. I turned around and turned the key.

'Adelaide!', said Mama. In her eyes was a bleak look I had not seen before. Some vengeance curling there perhaps, brought from its slumbers to dismay the day. 'The girls will hold her—Jane and Eveline'.

'AH!', came from Adelaide, but she was gripped, wrists held behind her back, I knew a conqueror, a warrior, emerge in me.

'Eveline, pull up her skirt!'—'YEE-OOOH!' came from her as I spoke, but then her thighs were bared, fringe of her muff. Pink stockings girded tightly up her thighs, pale bulb of bottom just a little shown. And all the room was still, was still.

'Let her be seen', said Pamela's companion. Hands extending, he drew up her skirts the more and bared all that was quite delectable to view—her quim well-thatched, thighs plumpish, pearly skin, her bottom naked and impertinent, well cleft for ventures she would now sustain.

'James will be first—then you', I said to him while Adelaide effected struggles, but no longer squealed. She clipped her thighs together. They were smacked by Eveline who knelt and bunched her fist between the girl's round knees. 'Papa also', I said, and added, 'But I do not wish to watch'. Their eyes were awed. Adelaide cried out my name in shrill despair. 'She will be tasted, as I would have been', I said, unlocked the door and slipped upstairs, my heart a-raging like a summer storm. I had undone myself perhaps. I heard a thin-pitched

45

cry and smiled, but held a moment to the bannisters. Mama would nip her with her teeth, perhaps. I did not really know the way of things, felt both despondent and yet proud. Adelaide had failed the test, had not been quiet. I knew instinctively one should be quiet, and on tiptoe to passion, as Papa had said.

I had not mentioned Arnold of deliberation—or I had forgot. It did not matter, anyway. I could not see his lips rimmed with her salt. His Mama would delay him from the deed, or mayhap hold him back. Imaginations of his withered penis in my mind.

I was a coward, so I told myself. I should have stayed and should have watched, yet had a slight distaste for orgies of that kind, however ceremonial they were. I did believe they were. Oddly enough, they have solemnity. The men's pricks rise, but are not shown. The girl is fêted afterwards with drinks, caresses, praise— all that, then order is restored and partners quietly chosen. This I learned in aftermath, but knew it also from an instinct that I had.

Some thirty minutes passed before I heard a footfall on the stairs. I knew its weight, I sensed its purpose, and sat still, my belly warm, my knees apart beyond the latitude of ladyhood. I waited on repentance and on hope. The door opened to admit my father-in-law.

'The girls will have you first—then I', he said. A small black whip hung down beside his thigh. The end was knotted and it twitched. I rose as if to greet him, but I did not smile. 'It is the price—the penalty', he said.

'In my own house?' I tried to stare him out, could not, and bowed my head a little. To his glee, I think.

'There will be others on your bed, between your thighs'.

'Mama will not permit'.

'She will be occupied, and is already so. Nests may be spermed today—it is the way of it. Remove your

46

gown and your chemise. You have no drawers on, I believe?'

'I have not, no'. My mood was moody, ever changeable. From earth I trod on swamp and then on earth again.

'Kneel well up on your bed and let your bottom overhang the edge. The whip will not lambast you overmuch, I swear'.

'And who prescribed this penalty?' I loosed my dress, began to draw it off. His eyes glowed at my nakedness beneath, my stockings taut as father had desired.

'Tradition, Emily—and there are others you will need to learn. My Lord, yes! I was told your legs were beautiful. Indeed they are. Turn round and show your bottom to me, girl'.

My gown discarded, I cast off my silk chemise and laid it on a chair, exposing as I turned my cleft cheeks to his wicked view.

'Superb! All that has been said of you is true. A perfect arse—a wondrous globe! Now, Emily, to the bed. Kneel up and place your hands before you as you do—and do so with a certain grace, I see, that well becomes your future. Legs apart, girl! Have you not been taught to show?'

I did not answer, hung my head, displayed my cleft, my quim, to him, and knew not why I did it and yet knew I must. His maleness was apparent in his stride, his stance, the bulge beneath his trousers, just as Papa was, and James, and Pamela's companion. I heard footsteps, heard a laugh from Adelaide, and then Papa's gruff tones. She uttered up a little 'Oh!', a girlish squeal, and was no doubt prepared to say her prayers.

ZOOO-WHITTT!, I heard, and then the whip's tip scorched my nether cheeks. I yelped, bucked forward, rocked. The sting was deep. It swirled across my bottom and explored the chasm, but before I could recover came another and another then, snake striking,

47

biting, a full flare of heat. I heard a wailing high inside my head and knew it to be mine, heard my thin screeches echo to the walls.

'D... don't!', I whimpered, but suppressed the 'please' I almost uttered, too. 'YEE-AAAARGH!' burst from my lips for even in my whimpering he coursed me twice again and caused my hips to swirl. The bed bounced underneath my knees. Tears plopping from my eyes fell on my hands. Redhot, white-hot, my bottom churned, and then his hands assailed me, held me still.

'Hold still, girl—keep your legs apart', he growled.

'I c... c... cannot!' But my howls ignored, he clamped me tighter, forced my hips to still, then suavely moved a finger up and down my groove, sought my rosette and felt the puckered rim.—'I am, I am, I am a bride', I moaned. I cared not what I said, and jittered, wriggled, as he urged his finger into my sleek channel, causing me to gasp.

'To all of us this day, I trust. Sustain it, Emily; you will have bigger there'.

'No, no! OOOH-AH!' His finger deeper up, I felt the knuckle and he twisted it quite gently, causing me to hiss and feel my rimmed rosette expand. His free hand seized upon my neck, forced my head down, nose buried in the quilt.

'Silence!', he uttered and I clenched my fists, swam in the darkness under eyelids that were closed, and snivelled as he moved his digit in and out. 'Now move your bottom back and forth, or you shall taste the whip more bitterly than you have known'.

'C... c... c... OOOH!', lips squashed, I choked and moved my bottom timidly, aware of dulled surrender in my mind and yet experiencing withal a sense of deep excitement to receive the probe.

'Straighten up now, Emily', I heard, and did so awkwardly. His finger half slipped out with the contraction of my bottom, but the tip remained. No sooner was my body straight than it urged within again and caused my legs to quiver, though I strove to keep them straight. My back was pressed against his broader form. His free arm stole around my waist and the hand descended slowly down my belly's curve to brush my thicket and then cup my quim.

'Turn your head now and extend your tongue to mine', he growled, his finger parting, as he spoke, the rolled lips of my cunny.

A whimper that was fretful sounded from my mouth—was followed by a quiet, submissive squeak as I was forced up on my toes by the insurgence of his finger in my bottomhole. My neck turned slowly and I found his mouth.

'How sweet your breath', he murmured, lips to lips. His tongue was broad and lapped my slimmer one. I sagged, was finger-thrust upright again, and—open-mouthed—felt swoony, trickling my saliva round his lips. A sound—creaking of door. Constance appeared, Fiona in her train. I struggled, wriggled, but was held, his mouth mashed deeper into mine, my neck a-strain, eyes wide and staring sideways at the pair.

'Tongue her, Fiona', came from Constance then. The young girl knelt before me and I made to clip my thighs. My lips were slippery beneath his own, neck twisted painfully. Fiona's head came up and forced my knees apart. His hand uncupped my cunny and her warm mouth buried up beneath, tongue sleeking into bubbling moisture there and causing me to gasp upon his breath the while that Constance fondled my hard nipples with her fingertips.

'Leave her to us, Papa; you promised'. Constance said. Her tongue lisped long and wet between our own while Fiona's found my perky spot and maddened it.

'Do not be long about it then, for we must have

49

her home with us. Bring her submissive to the carriage when you do'.

'What else?' asked Constance. No sooner had his wicked finger plopped from out my bottom cheeks, and he unfolding me, than she whipped round to take his place and brought her arms beneath my armpits and so held me thus. I stared at him glaze-eyed and jittered, mewed, as Fiona's tongue extolled my spurting juices, gently caressing up and down my stockinged thighs with her soft hands.

'Quite beautiful. Arnold chose well', he said.

'*Papa*! He did not chose her—Mama did, as you well know. Pray leave us to our privacies. Jane is not finished with as yet, and nor is Eveline. If you would. . . .'

'Yes'.

I struggled as he went, to no avail, was pressed and dragged upon my bed, and such a twisting, wrestling then occurred, all silent, with my puffing, that I scarce knew where I was—whose legs were whose. Constance inverted herself, face down into my belly and her calves around my neck. The pair then rolled me on my hip, Fiona's tongue a-working at my bottom and that of her sister underneath my cunnylips.

'GOO-GOOO!', I choked to no avail. Twin tongues invaded me. That of Fiona sleeked within my rosette while she sprang my cheeks apart. I tried to free my head but I could not. My belly rippled and I came again, saltspray upon the mouth of Constance, and she lapping greedily. I seized my pillow, bit into its plump white surface, strained my legs and came and came again. . . .

CHAPTER 7

I slept. Defensively I slept and yet it was a slumber brief but deep. The bottom sheet was sticky under me as I awoke, saw Jane. She bent to me and kissed my brow. I scanned the room for my assailants, then sank back again.

'Was it nice?', she asked with laughter in her voice, drew down the bedclothes, saw my swollen nipples, brown on cream, and sighed. 'It looks to be; we are all tidy now. You may get up. Come, let me brush your hair'.

'I hate them all', I bleated. Quite exhausted from my spillings, I had not even felt myself put into bed.

'Pleasure can be resented, I suppose, if it should come from those we do not like, and yet. . . . Pleasure is pleasure, darling. Once you have succumbed, you may again'.

'Shut up!', I blurted, then sat up and swung my legs from out the bed. My stockings were all wrinkled up. 'Did *you*?', I asked her pertly, and got up, having my naked bottom patted with affection as I did.

'Oh, as to *that* . . . but do get dressed. We are all tidied, as I said, and all is orderly by now. No one will remark upon your absence. When penalties are to be paid, the bill is often quickly offered up, and best it were it should be paid without remorse. I never really have remorse myself—not when my cunny tingles still'.

'I don't doubt that', I mumbled, but she tickled me, caused me to giggle all despite myself, then saw to my attire and helped me dress. 'The world is upside down', I said.

'Oh, silly, it is never that, but *we* are, sometimes. When you are trestled, then you really feel it so'.

'Trestled?', I asked, sat at my dressing table while she brushed my hair.

'Oh, I forgot, of course, how distant you have been to some things here. Yes, Emily, a trestle with a cushion on the top. There is one in the corner of the stable you have never seen. Covered with green baize it is when not in use. When hung upon it, one's legs dangle down, bottom upraised and head hung low. Impossible to touch the floor with toes or reaching fingers, though one tries. And then the tawse—maybe the cane or birch—stings deep into one's nether cheeks and . . . OOOH!'

Her hips wriggled as she spoke. I stared at her reflection in the glass, suppressed the utterance I might have made and said instead, 'Oh, Jane, please stay with me!'

'In your new, married state, my love? Did you hear what Constance did to Arnold downstairs—oh! How docile he becomes in female hands! His prick is really *reedy*, darling, thin and long. Perfect for bottom-tupping, though! Stay with you? May I? Yes, my love. Mama said that I might; I *asked*, you see. She had the thought of it already in her heart, and Papa . . .'

'*What*? What did he say?'

'That we might take such roads as we may find. He is persuaded of our good sense and our carefulness— did not say so in such words, but I read it in his eyes'.

'You read as well as I, Jane!'—Papa's voice. He entered, closed the door, stood with his back to it. I heard a scuttering of feet outside and knew it to be Adelaide returning from devotions, no doubt dressed again. The thought was catty, and I stroked its fur. Hers would be moist. Were we then somehow kin, or were all females so beneath the skin?

'Jane is brushing my hair', I mumbled like a child.

'And well she does it, Emily. As to you, my love,

the trap is closed and yet is open. Such are the paradoxes we encounter in the world'.

I sprang up, and the hairbrush clattered down.

'Why did you make me, then—why did?', I flared at him. Gold-ringed, my slim heart-finger waved in a remonstrance.

'May I sit down?', he asked and took a chair close to the dressing table, knees against my knees. 'I have to tell you now, to tell you both, that our finances are not quite what they once were. Your father-in-law is wealthy and will shower you with delights, as I cannot henceforth. And Jane will be no less well-served, I'm sure.'

I gaped, knees slackening. Jane stared at him as well.

'You mean, we would be poor?', I asked.

'Not quite—not that. Not that as yet, at least. We shall retain the house, dismiss a servant here and there, but you have need, my pets, of furs and dresses, ball-gowns, fancy underclothes and jewelry—all that becomes young ladies of your class'.

'I do not need...' I clenched my fists.

'*I* do', said Jane, and laughed the tinkling laugh she always laughs, one with no malice in it but a summer's chime.

'Oh, *you*', said I. Papa rose, took my hand, said many were the roads that led to Rome. His eyes were just a trifle tearful, so I thought, but took it for a trick of light.

'Arnold is foppish, weak. Your allowances—yes, for you both—I have arranged already. They are large. You will neither of you need to wheedle for the things that you will need, my dear. A covenant is signed, the ink is dry'.

'You mean, Papa, that we are being sold', I said. I turned my back to him. He spun me around again. I thought of his discovery of James and me and felt un-kind. He had not birched me as he might have done.

'All things have price. One pays with words or ges-tures, gifts, or kind, yet we lose nothing in the giving if we give with a free heart. Is that not so?'

He drew me to him, kissed me on the mouth in sight of Jane.

'I do not know', I mumbled, pulled my lips away, stared at the floor but clutched still at his arms.

'Perhaps . . .', said Jane. She stopped; she had no words to follow her *perhaps*. A laugh, a crash of glasses from downstairs, brought us apart, I fiddling with my dress and silent then. I had a need to be caressed, my bottom to be soothed; it fretted me. Stir of my hips; they saw my hips a-stir. Jane breathed out softly; Papa turned away, moved to the door and hesitated, as he often did when in my room.

'*Perhaps*—yes. All things are perhaps', he said.

'We shall come down', said Jane. Her tone was crisp, brought order to my mind, a suddenness of some decision that I gathered up.

'My room—I wish it kept', I said.

'Of course. What else?' He gazed at me, was gone. I touched my wardrobe, knew its old, blank stare. The long and time-stained mirrors on the door, surrounded by fancy scrolls of wood, would hold my image ever on. When someone stood before them, they would see me there.

All was propriety downstairs, as Jane had said. Only two cushions tossed upon the floor showed evidence of wanton play. I wished to examine them as might a scientist, but went to Mama and received a kiss. Her lips were over-moist, as too were Eveline's. Arnold stood pale and wan, top-hat in hand. I could not imagine him with riding crop, as Papa sometimes carried, nor a gun. Farewells were said, James kissed me on the eyes, which I thought sweet. His trousers were not fully buttoned, though, were twisted at the front where he, in haste, had missed a buttonhole. I whispered to him so; he blushed.

'Come, chaperone', I said to Jane. I had a merriment of slight hysteria. All stared at first, then laughed in turn.

'I will take your arm', said Arnold. Suddenly he came to life. His Papa, I believe, had frowned at him.

'No, thank you, Arnold, I have Jane's', I said. Our bodies moved like leaves that drift in a slow breeze. The servants bowed to me upon the steps, the sunlight—dreaming of past summers—shone. 'The carriage is not clean', I said to Arnold. Jane sat with me of a purpose, and he forced to face us both.

'Ah, no', he uttered—had no more to say, save for such spinnings in his mind as might occur but could not, would not be produced. The gravel chinked and grated underneath the wheels as our procession moved. Mama waved, Papa waved, and Eveline. Julie had not come, alas, though much had wanted to, had been transported off to Paris, but would soon return. I wondered if she had said her prayers in French these past few days, and were her stockings straight, as mine had been.

'Shall we play croquet later, do you think?', Jane asked. I stared at her, and Arnold gaped. 'Two balls and a stiff stick', she murmured in my ear, then bit the lobe of it, made me say 'Ouch!'

'I say!', said Arnold. —'Oh, be quiet', said Jane to him. I laughed; the laughter welled up from within, threw my head back till tears came in my eyes and Arnold's face became a perfect blur such as I wished it ever to remain.

CHAPTER 8

Some houses have little to be said of them, except they stand foursquare and have sufficient greenery to flirt and flow around their stolid walls, shrubs flourishing, upstarting trees, and sad, brown borders that lament the deaths of flowers when Autumn comes.

Arnold's—I should say his father's, rather—was imposing, turreted in the fond manner of an architect who believes the Crusades still to be unfinished.

Armoured, hollow men stood in the hall. All looked baronial and overdone. I did not like the crossed assegais on the walls, the hide shields. The stuffed birds were nice.

'We shall have pleasant days here', Constance said. Arnold dispersed himself upstairs. The drawing room was langourous and grand with silk and braided chairs, a crimson ottoman, a fine old Davenport.

'It may be so', I answered cautiously. Her Mama, Hilda, weighed me up and down and smiled. Jane fiddled with some cut flowers, looked about, and had an air on her as if she did not mind the place.

My room—I had my own room, as it seemed— was next to that of Constance who then guided me around. 'The beds squeak sometimes—are you used to that?', she asked.

'I am, yes', I replied and stared her out, at which her eyes dropped, disconcerted, as I thought.

'We favoured you with lips and tongues', she said and then embraced me quickly as if I might retreat. I did not fold my arms defensively between us and was kissed upon my eyelids just as James had done. How easy it becomes to tell ourselves sometimes that such and such a one is nice when they are not! I wished to say she had outraged me, though in aftermaths I never bleat.—'You are delicious to make love with—did you know?', she asked.

'You know much more about it than I do—or seemingly. Where, then, is Arnold?'

'He? He will be seen to. Do not fret as to his cause. He has his weaknesses; I know them well.'

'I'm sure you do'. I turned my back on her and fiddled with the curtains. Velvet green they were, and not quite to my taste. Quite unabashed, she came behind me, licked her tongue around my neck.

'I am not incestuous, Emily. D'you think I am?'

'I care not...', I began, and then her Mama came in. I felt the smile of Constance on my neck together with her pointed tongue that made me quiver-tickle-tingle all at once. Her arms around my waist, my bottom bulbed into her belly, still she did not move.

'Shall you play maid at tea, or Emily, or Jane?', she asked.

'I? No—I did it yesterday, Mama, or was it last week? So much happens here'.

'Last week? Last year? Your legs were much admired. Dear Emily, she does not know of what we speak, though. Let her choose between herself and Jane. It is her day'.

'It is? I had scarce noticed it', I said. The sun's rays were stooping shallow on the lawn. A blackbird uttered its bright song.

'She has a touch of humour on her, Mama, does she not—it is very sweet. You *are* sweet; did you know that, Emily?' She turned me—all were fit, it seemed, to turn me as they would. I wished to beat at her, at her brown dress. Instead, I laughed, and thought myself a fool: a weakness in me I could not disperse. In their strange commonness, bizarre of tongue, was a rough strand of jollity that meant not to offend.

Hilda departing, Constance stroked my face. Fingers of velvet, yes, she had.

'You have not played "maid"?', she asked. 'It is not so common in the county here. Papa says it is not, at least. A girl is dressed up as a servant girl, but with a skirt that shows her legs, and with an unstarched blouse with buttons all undone. She serves, we toy with her, then Arnold takes his pleasure of her. Such he is allowed to do. Papa may spank her first, though—make her ready for the cock. Are you cock-ready, darling? Tell me yes!'

'I have . . . I have been. Does he—does he do it in your sight?'. I wanted not to know, and yet I did. Pressed to the wall she kept me, and our thighs were warm. Julie would come and tongue us both, perhaps. Mad thoughts invaded me—I in this house, this strange room, with its camphor smell, the scent of polish redolent on wood.

'That is for you to say—or rather, it is now'.

'I have a choice?' Sullen my mouth. I altered it and smiled. Tomorrow I would flee with Jane, I told myself. It mattered not as to the evening or the night.

'Of course, you silly. Is not love here shared? I will play a little with his cock. I promise you, I do no more than that. He is so timid really, one can handle him at will. His prick bursts in long, fine-spurting flood. Surprising, really, that he does so much. Ah, Fiona— yes, come in—what do you say? Shall it be Emily or Jane to play the maid today?'

'Neither', said I, and hooked her stare. 'You said the choice was mine—so be it. Fiona here shall play the part. Dress the girl quickly and be done with it. I would soon as see this play as any other'.

'But I don't want! Oh, not with Arnold, no!', Fiona uttered, pouting, shifting feet, tugging at dress.

59

'Fiona, she has never watched before. It is her due to see—today. Another time, another place, all will be different. Once and only once—you will for me?', so Constance wheedled, but I then stood firm, said it was my wish and not hers. At that, Fiona turned and ran downstairs, I following and Constance in my wake.

'The maid is Fiona', I announced. The congregation was complete: Arnold, his parents, and my sister sat as though all waiting for a train.

'You take command?', her father asked, his eyes amused, his mouth a line of doubtfulness. He lounged in shirtsleeves—a very common touch—as Arnold did, their collars off.

I felt then in the long, ensuing hour that I had wandered on a stage—in view of audience—where an unwritten play was to be performed. Some altercation had ensued, but Fiona finally was sent upstairs, was dressed her part, and came down with a vague attempt at shyness, on her own. A skirt, much cut, of dusty black, came to her stocking tops which, like a servant's, were of the same hue. Unbuttoned was her blouse: the halfmoons showed. Her hair was caught up with a ribbon tightly tied.

'Serve me. I will have port—the others, too', her father said and winked at me a vulgar wink that I ignored. Too long she was about it and was fetched by Jane who did not mind the chore and afterwards confessed to me that she had felt the girl a little, found no drawers, and 'tickled up her pussy just for larks'.

Fiona was flushed when she came in, found us expectant, served her Papa first. I wondered at his hand that hovered near her thighs. He did not touch, though, and merely smiled. Arnold did neither, for I stared him out. Hilda sniffed at her glass and rose. The night would be long, she said, and drifted off to go upstairs.

'Do you wear drawers, you naughty servant girl?', asked Constance of her sister when it came her turn to take a glass.—'No', said Fiona pettishly and made to make her exit, but her sister caught her wrist. I suspected some contraction of the action that might normally obtain—yet in all truth they had not the finesse for it.

Erotic moments, as I have long learned, must be played slowly, rather as a string quartet expands a melody as if to say, 'We may not finish here today'. Knees should be shown, the stocking tops displayed, a rim of thigh above—no more than that. First kisses should be soft, exploratory, the bottom rolling, wiggling, as one walks. Hands may explore the tits outside the dress, but not within. A bedroom may be entered, but one sits at first, with thighs displayed, upon a sofa, toying with a prick not yet revealed to one, with fingers languorous—not too excited then—around one's quim.

In such a mood, I have been come upon long since by a maidservant, but I did not stay my caressing hand, nor he. The girl looks slyly, sideways, at the pair. If she is clever, skilled at boudoir games, she may dust around a little, even humming to herself, and then depart— perhaps have glimpsed at last the lady's legs apart and seen her fondly tickled muff, the gentleman's stiff prick displayed. The couple may ignore her presence or, if the maid is pretty, may then call her back into the room and invite her to join them on the waiting bed.

'No drawers? Why, how provocative! Go to the gentleman you first served, then, and ask his pardon for your rude display', said Constance to her sister who, hesitating, was ordered to put down her tray, given a push, and wandered with her finger in her mouth to her Papa.

'Yes?', he enquired.—'I have no d . . . d . . . drawers on sir', said she.

'Is your bottom, then, so warm you do not need to wear them? Let me see it; lie face down across my lap'.

'Oh no, Papa—I mean, sir—please!' A real wail from Fiona. Was it real?

He seized her wrist and made her tumble down, face forward, belly on his thighs, and flipped her skirt up. The black stockings made her thighs above gleam sweetly.

'No, no!', she shrieked as he uncovered her and brought her bottom to our view.

Chubby the cheeks were, plump with girlishness, the chasm tight. I could not resist the sudden thought that it invited explorations. Her ankles were towards us. Bent far over as she was, palms flat upon the carpet, one could see her nest, the peeping fig of the tight cunnylips.

'Sir, please—oh, not too hard!', she cried, then SMACK! His palm descended on her rumptious cheeks and brought a wailing cry from her, a pink flare showing on the snow-white hemispheres.

'Harder!', called Constance. Sitting on the ottoman with me, she ringed my waist and made me lean to her, our cheeks together. Thinking that I might be next, I made no struggle, watched his hand rise and descend again, bringing a juicy splatting sound and yet another sobbing cry. Her hips bounced and her fingers dug into the carpet. Arnold—who had a frontal view with Jane—gazed open-mouthed but otherwise was limp as washing on a line. My sister's hands moved up and down her thighs, her knees apart, a flush upon her face.

'WAH-HAAAR! Oh, Papa, not so hard!', shrieked the young, shapely victim while the tongue of Constance licked around my mouth and brought my yielding tongue to seek her own. A warmth was in my belly, and a mood of devilment. SMACK! SMACK!—'GOO-HOOO!' from Fiona. Each time she closed her legs, he smacked her thighs and made her quim to show the more. Jane uttered a huge sigh, lay back and moved her bottom on the seat, watching the maiden's hot-smacked derriere as it bumped up and down. Her arm-chair being next to Arnold's, she extended her hand to his, but when his did not move she drew it back again and gave me an excited, guilty look.

'BOO-HOOO!', Fiona sobbed. Her bottom was bright pink. Her legs went of a sudden limp. Her father's hand then raised up high again but descended very slowly and came to rest in seeming benediction on her quivering cheeks.

'You should see to her', he said to Constance. His lips looked thicker and his face was flushed. Fiona uttered up a wail and rolled like a rag doll from off his lap to settle on her tummy on the floor. She sobbed and sneezed, and then lay still again, legs spread.

'Help me take her upstairs, Emily. Arnold, you will follow us', said Constance.

'NO-HO, don't want to!', Fiona sobbed and drew her legs up, rolled into a ball, but Constance rose and roughly pulled her up, skirt hitched, her glowing bottom showing red.

'Come, Miss! Recalcitrance will only bring you more', said Constance, dragging on her wrist and beckoning me to take Fiona's other arm. Jane got up, too, and said that she would come. Before she could move again, however, Fiona's father lumbered up and went across to her and whispered something in her ear, then said aloud, 'It is the custom that one girl should stay'.

Fiona was struggling, but we got her to the door while Arnold, getting up reluctantly, came in our wake. Over my shoulder I saw Jane being led towards the ottoman our bottoms had left warm. I knew, however, that her look was fey—not so dismayed as she would have me think. I somehow recognised those seemingly grudging footsteps that she took—have often seen it since in other girls who wish one to believe they do not want to play.

I heard her 'OOOH!' sound as we entered the wide hall. Fiona, kicking, needed to be dragged.

'Arnold, pick up her legs—we'll carry her', snapped Constance.—'NO-WOH!', squealed Fiona, but we did, all five feet three of her slung in our arms, her bared legs threshing feebly while Arnold made a funny hissing sound. His face was pale, not flushed as others' would have been. To her own room we carried her.—'Fiona, you will obey, you know you must', said Constance as the door was closed, 'Get on the bed, Miss, bottom up, or Papa will bring the birch to you'.

'Not fair—it's not!', Fiona whimpered. Even so, she kneed her way upon the bed, presenting her cleft orb upon whose surfaces the red had paled a little to a glossy pink.

'Hold her head down, Emily; she likes much to be held. Now, Arnold, take your boots and trousers off. Your bride is watching, dear—perform with grace', Constance commanded. How absurd, bizarre, the tableau was, yet I absorbed it as one does a book that captures the imagination, draws one into mystery from page to page and will not be put down until a climax has obtained.

Arnold obeyed. First he unlaced his boots then cast them off. Giving a wretched look at me, who stood with hand upon Fiona's neck, he worked his trousers down and then at last displayed his penis to my view, his shirt tucked up by Constance whose hands were motherly, not lewd as I expected. Some eight inches long, his thin, stiff penis had erected, spirelike, with a purplish knob much like unto a very fat acorn.

'Em . . . Emily. . . .', he stammered. Constance then took hold of it, her fingers closely ringed around the root, and pulled him till his knees were at the bed.

'How like a hound he is! Some large, slim-bodied dogs have pricks the like. Do you not think so, Emily? He is exercised in this way once a week. Mama says it may weaken him to do it more. Do you think it would? His balls are a fair size, though, are they not?'

Arnold stood quivering as she spoke, thin-thighed, and belly flat as is a girl's. His pubic hairs were sandy. I remarked that fact with distant eyes. He stared down at his younger sister's upraised bottom as though it might be an offered bun. Fiona squeaked, head-twisting, but I held her down.

Not receiving a reply from me, Constance made Arnold take his stance upon the bed, smacked Fiona's calves to make them open more while his knees shuffled inbetween, his poker rising up against her cheeks.

'Remark well, dear Emily—although I am sure that you already know—that a girl who has been spanked or birched or caned or tawsed—must have her bottom cooled by a syringe. Arnold's is quite perfect for the task, is quite exquisite when it urges up', said Constance and with that she bent his prick little down and pointed it at Fiona's pinky-brown and wrinkled nether hole.

'HOOO-AAAR! Oh no!', Fiona squealed.

'Be quiet, girl!', came from me, to my surprise. I held her head with both hands—Constance held her hips. Arnold uttered a gasping sound and infiltrated his warm, swollen knob into her offered aperture, at which her back dipped. Artfully, her bottom balled more thus, encouraging his entry. Peering then, I saw three inches of his cock glide in, and she a-wriggle, though not with much force.

'No, no, no, don't', she wailed. The cry was token, though. His mouth was slack and wobbly and I cared not for the sight of it. James had looked flushed but quite angelic when he fingered up my bottomhole. I had permitted that. I had known the first sweet stinging of the probe that brought a rich and sickly feel of plea-sure in its wake. Had Papa not come in, I might have yielded.

65

'T . . . t . . . t . . . tight!', came Arnold's groan. He grimaced, Fiona moaned and bit her fist.

'Get into her, you fool, and work her well', said Constance.

'Ah!', he uttered sharply and, with that, rooted himself in her delicious derriere until I sensed his balls were hanging underneath her nest.

'Mama, Mama!', Fiona squeaked. Her hips squirmed, jerked a little, then were still.

'Play with her titties now—bend over her. She has to do it now—it is the rule', said Constance. She released her sister's hips and beckoned me to take my hands away in turn. Then she embraced me, drew me aside to watch, her warm cheek pressed to mine.— 'Come sideways, you will better see', she said, and gathered up my dress in folds to feel my garters and my thighs. Arnold was puffing as he worked his loins. His palms scooped out Fiona's melons, nipples sprouting from between his fingers.

'OOOH-WOOH!', she sobbed, his belly smacking to her bottom as they threshed, the long stiff penis almost full emerging and then ploughing in again. I watched. My eyes were hot, my lips were moist. SLAP-SMACK!—SLAP-SMACK!—the moans, the choked-off cries, the hot cork gliding in and out.

'Have you watched before? You have not—have you—have not watched before?', asked Constance softly, and pulled up my dress to bare my bottom and my thatch. My mouth did not wish to kiss hers, did not wish her sharp saliva, nor her hand that cupped the plump mound of my quim, and yet, and yet, my lips were under hers, she easing fingers back and forth to make me tremble.—'What a luscious honeypot you have, dear Emily. Part your legs the more and flex your knees. There, there! You cannot help yourself! Who can? Now look again. He'll cream her bottom soon.

The little witch will suck him dry, I know. Quick, kiss her Emily, the while he does!'

'WAH!' This time the short, soft cry was mine. Pushed, bundled down, face under Fiona's—my legs a-dangle on the floor—I drew the girl's mouth down upon my own. O sweet it was, so small, so soft, so moist. Her tongue slid like an uncoiled spring between my lips, her moans resounding as she bucked, and Arnold's fierce, quiet hissing heard above. SPLATT! smacked her bottom into him. Then Constance knelt and thrust her face between my thighs and brought her tongue to soothe around my slit, causing my knees to hang upon her shoulders as she did.

Ah, whirl of memories—the pants, the moans, the liquid sounds we made! My bottom bounced on the bed's edge. I flooded the warm, seeking mouth of Constance while Fiona gargled, twirled her tongue to mine, then uttered a thin cry of animal delight as Arnold groaned and loosed his sperm deep up her clenching bottomhole.

'Children! What are you playing at?', I heard.

And no one moved, and no one moved.

'We are playing, Mama. Go away!', said Constance from between my legs.

'I see you are, indeed. Do not be long. Tea will be shortly served. Or supper—is it supper? I am now not sure'.

The door closed, and we were alone again.

CHAPTER 9

'Go away', said I. I had forgotten for a moment that the
room was not my own. Constance rose and wiped her
lips.

'You will soon be the same as us', she said.

I turned my face away and brooded at the wall,
heard a faint plopping sound as Arnold drew his penis
out. Released from off the cork, Fiona sighed a sigh of
some contentment and then settled down, moving her
tummy like a cat upon the coverlet. Arnold was bidden
to leave. I wished him to before I turned my head in
his direction. Rustling trousers, picking up his boots,
he slouched without, his ammunition spent.

Too much had stirred in me. Remembering where
I was, I left the room without a word and found my
own abode, though it felt merely like another ornate
cave, a place of strangeness, as the whole house was.
Making to close my door, I felt a hand beyond against
it, opened it anew, and there was Jane.

'PHEW!', she laughed and threw herself upon my
bed, eyes wide and wanting me to ask that which I did
not wish to ask.

'Jane, I wish to leave'.

'To leave?' She sat bolt upright, hands behind her
hips and stared.

There is no comfort here. Do you find comfort
here?', I asked, then voices sounded from below and I
moved to the window and opened it with the same wan
hope that one awaits the returning of a carriage late at
night when a loved one is despaired of. Some madness

in me asked if it were James or Papa, come with rescue ropes and mattresses to leap upon.

'Who? What?', asked Jane, and I thought her, in our sisterhood, to be of the same frame of mind, but one she would not bring herself to speak. I waved my hand and shushed her. Down below a gentleman of fair appearance stood, conversing with a gardener.

'Soor—why, yes—you goes along the same road as you took, turns left by Frencham's barn—stands on its own, it does—goes half a mile up there, and there you are, and Bob's yer uncle as they say, soor. Thankee, soor', the servant uttered, pocketing a coin, whereat the gentleman was about to turn away when I leaned out and called 'Hallo!'

'Madam?', he responded, and his eyes looked bright the moment he looked up. Jane tugged at me and giggled, but I would not yield.

'Are you going to the Hall?', I asked, making him to blink against the sky.

'The Hall? By jove, I am! Would you then come?'

'If you can accommodate my sister also, sir—yes, gladly. We have need of a conveyance. Can you wait upon us just five minutes?'

'Five will be splendid. Six would be eternity, from what I see of you'.

'Emily, we cannot!', Jane flustered as I drew the window to.

'Then you may stay. I will not a pass a night within this house, nor would Mama allow you to, if she but knew'.

'Oh, Emily, but . . .'

'No buts, now, for I mean to go. Quick, get your reticule, your cloak. Our clothes will be sent on—they have to be'.

'Oh, Emily!' Her cry was such as made her seem my junior then, but with a flourish of uncertain eyes, wild hands, she went, and met me on the landing in

70

a trice, cloak over arm and reticule tight held, as though it might be snatched. 'They will see us, Emily!'—and panic in her voice.

'What if they do? We are not prisoners, are we? May we not go out to greet an old friend passing by? Follow me quietly, dear, and make no sound'.

Rustling of skirts! How loud they sound in circumstances such, though one has no consciousness of them otherwise. The hollow, armoured men stood waiting on a battle that would never come again. The door to the drawing room was but ajar. We heard the small, smug clink of china and then hastened to the far front door. It rattled as I opened it.

'See who that is', called Hilda's voice.

'Oh, God!', said Jane, and ran and ran with me along the gravel sidepath to the gentleman who stared in some surmise at our approach until I lightly touched his arm, and then he smiled.

'Someone is beckoning', he said. I turned and saw a maid who waved her arm uncertainly.

'She is inopportune', I said. I felt it my *bon mot*, and had my arm possessively clasped in turn.

'Are we not all!', he laughed. His eyes were in mine as he spoke, not at my bosom, nor my thighs. The maid squeaked something, like a nightjar that has lost its voice. I waved to her as though to say, 'Indeed! It is a good day, is it not?', then we walked on to where his carriage stood.

Introductions were effected as we got within. His name was Harry Marminter. I judged him to be thirty-five or thereabouts. He had a jolly air on him, but yet beneath a strain of seriousness. He was beardless, with a small moustache, and as fair-looking as a man might be who does not swell his paunch with beer, nor carry a red nose for whisky's sake.

'You are to visit Aramintha?', he then asked. His

wedding ring and the familiar tone he used indicated to me that she was his wife.

'She is well?', I responded. I had not, after all, said yes, and Jane sat frozen, with a frozen smile that did not, however, betoken an ill-ease but more dumbfoundedness.

'Indeed, but shy as ever. How extra-*ordinary* we three have not met before. Your carriages are in repair?'

I caught a narrowing of his eyes, and laughed.

'They are—but we are not', I riposted and fell to talking of the weather, and all nonsense such, with such relief upon me as the poor folk of Lucknow must have felt, for I sensed a ring of honesty in him that nowadays is rare to come by even in the Shires.

'How did you *know*—about the Hall, I mean?', Jane whispered to me urgently when we arrived. The house was quite a small one by our standards, had the look of an old Vicarage.

'Know what? I say, forgive my rudeness, but you both intrigue me much. Two pretty sisters without chaperone are not too often seen—I do regret', said Harry.

'Sir, I must confess to you . . . But pray, no, let us come in first, if enter still we may. We are but fugitives of overwrought desire', I told him as the entrance door came near. 'A guess, you fool. It had to be a Manor or a Hall', I whispered to my sister, who then looked contrite.

The hallway had a bareness to it in comparison with the baronial manor we had left: rush matting on the parquet floor, an ornate coatstand, a deer's head with dusty antlers, an oval, gilded mirror—that was all. A maid, a young girl, scuttled from a side room, wiped her hands upon her apron, and then curtseyed to the master, which was rare, and so I thought him of high station.

'Mistress is in her boudoir, sir'.

72

'We shall attend upon her then. Bring wine up for our guests'.

'The red or white, sir?'

'Both, you ninnikins! Come, ladies, let us greet the Mistress of the house—then shall your tale be told. I trust it is diverting. Both of us have quite a taste for the unusual. Aramintha! I bring orphans from the storm!', he bellowed up the stairs, but in such good humour that I took much more to him. The stairs were thinly carpeted. Our footsteps sounded as we went, and the staircase was a fairly narrow one, so we three went in file, with Jane behind me, and he leading up.

'Orphans? Females, I trust?'

The languid and soft voice came from a bedroom just along the corridor above. Entering, we found a lady on the bed of much the same age as our host. She wore a pale blue peignoir and her stockings showed together with the bows and frills of a chemise. Her hair was corngold, her eyes were beautiful. Upon our entrance she leaned up and cast aside a book, yawning and covering her mouth as though to say, 'I did not mean to yawn'.

'My dears!', she said, but made no move to rise until, it seemed, she had absorbed us fully with her eyes, came to herself and gasped, 'I am not dressed for visitors! Harry, pray entertain them in the drawing room'.

'Of course, my pet'.

We were again led out—a quite bizarre occasion, as I thought and descended as might ones who had come to the wrong house, though Harry—being courteous—annulled our obvious dismay.

'You know how shy she is—or perhaps you do not?', he enquired, we meeting the maid upon the stairs and she then turning round, descending in her turn, and all our actions as might have graced a farce.

'It is we, sir, who have explanations to make. I am

a fleeing bride', said I, whereat his eyebrows raised, and then he laughed.

'Most that I know hasten only to their marital beds to take their pleasure, Miss, Mrs. . . .'

'You may call me Emily'.

Not wishing to betray Papa—and Jane with slightly worried, warning looks at me, I gave him hints of my past treatment, veiling much, but quite unable to dissemble all. Before I had finished my halting narrative, Aramintha joined us, bearing not a little of mystery herself.

'He finds me always—always finds me—don't you, Harry? Picking up my trail here, there. It is a game we play, you know. This is my aunt's house; she is absent for the season. The poor dear has scarce a thousand sovereigns to rub together, so I pay her rent. Which reminds me, dearest, that you owe me fifty. Your rings are nice, my dear. May I, too, call you by your Christian names? I heard from up above; I could not help. Marriage is such a bore. I know not why I married Harry. Look—he blushes!'

And to my surprise, he did.

'We master each other—taking turns, in fact; that is the trick of it. Being of equal strength of mind, we have no problem as to that. Married this morning and already fleeing, Emily? I envy you your courage! Of course, my own circumstances were quite other. My dear Harry. . . .'

But before she could continue there was a loud knocking at the door, at which I started, as did Jane.

'Your new-found kin?', asked Harry. He got up, went to a cabinet and thence drew out sword and flourished it and made the light from its fine blade to flash, causing my sister and I considerable astonishment.— 'One never opens one's front door to unknown visitors in such secluded areas', he said, 'without a weapon in one's hand'.

74

'Particularly if it is a lady, and then he bares his own', laughed Aramintha, but even as she said it covered up her mouth with the prettiest of gestures. While Harry strode into the hall, I wished that the floor would swallow me, as well did Jane.

'Sir?', came the voice of Harry in the entrance hall.

'Sir, I believe you have my son's new bride here'. And, as will be guessed, it was my father-in-law.

'There is a young lady of some repute who may be such. She is our guest, and not on sufferance. Need I say more? I bid you good day, sir. Your presence is unwelcome here, will not be suffered, and is not to be repeated. Unless, of course, you are invited, which I doubt would be the case'.

'Look here! I say!'

'A strange thing to say, indeed. I have no cause to look, and no desire. Pray notice that my sword has a fine edge to it and would trim your coat to tatters if you tried to enter'.

'I shall bring help, sir—village constables!'

'There is but one. He likes his port, I know, and often quaffs a glass here at the servant's door. Emily! You wish to leave?'

I skipped my way across the carpet and peered through the door along the hall. The bluff face stared into my own. His way was barred.

'I do not, no. Papa will be here shortly and will see me home—thanks to the message I have sent him', I replied, and lied more glibly than I knew I could.

'You have your answer, sir—begone!', said Harry, and then closed the door. A shout was heard of uttermost dismay. As Harry turned away, the letterbox was opened, and my father-in-law's voice—more strangulated than I was wont to hear—called through that Arnold would be woebegone.

'He is already—underneath his trousers mostly', I replied, then flushed a little at my daring and retreated.

Aramintha laughed and rose and kissed my cheek. I envied her composure that she had not stirred before.

'Is that the real reason that you left?', she asked.

'I think it not', said Harry. Entering, he closed the door. 'You did not hear all, my dear. The girls were rousted—playfully perhaps, but with too much gusto, and too soon. Arnold did his duty by his sister, not his bride'.

'Really? Oh, what excitement! Did he do her in your sight?', she asked.

'The world is full of strangeness, Aramintha, as are dreams'. I thought of what Papa has said about the latter, but could not spin out his words.

'Oh, DO go on! I really am shy, but I love to hear of naughtiness. You mean, you only dreamt it, or you saw it done? I have hidden behind screens myself and seen the *wickedest* of things. Do you remember, Harry...? Oh, but Emily, you tell us first'.

'Yes, do', said Jane. She had always loved to try and egg me on, and saw her chance for it.

'He is a plaything for his sisters, that is all, and—weakling as he is—is cozened by his Mama. I suspect her to have made him come herself. I would not put it past her now. He had his younger sister on her bed, and bottom-up she was'.

'By jove, he corked her!', Harry interrupted and thus saved me from saying it.

'Such things are done, but not on the first *day* of marriage—heavens, no!', said Aramintha, as though such things were absolutely *de rigueur* unless they happened afterwards: a decent interval—perhaps two days, or three, I thought sarcastically, and yet I warmed to her. Her eyes were warm, her tone was kind.

Had I really sent for my Papa, she asked, and I confessing that I had not, we were invited as 'eternal guests', this meaning, so she said, that once we had taken hospitality beneath her roof, we might do so for evermore. The following night there would be guests, she added, whereupon both Jane and I declared our lack of right attire.

'Harry will see to it. Take Jenkins, dearest, he is somewhere lurking, as he ever is', said she to him, whereat her husband drew upon a bellcord, summoned in the maid, demanded tea and the appearance of the said one. In two minutes he appeared—a giant of a man with lumbering stride, cap held in both his hands. His eyes appeared not to notice Jane and I, but I felt us both well taken in. His manly bulge was heavy underneath rough trouser cloth.

'How long have you been with me, Jenkins? Ten inches, is it? Oh no, I beg the pardon of all here! I had intended to say *months*, of course. The master has a job for you. A little journey and a stern stand such as you produce always upon demand. There are valises, trunks, to be procured, belonging to these young ladies. These together with a maiden of the household, I should say. Constance is her name. Your master will say her presence is required by Emily and Jane. Now you may go. Wait in attendance, quaff your beer.'

'Yes, m'am. I will that, m'am. And thankee m'am'.

'What?', I began, but tea was served. I waited for the maid to go.

'Why, simple is it not? I have taken into care young ladies in the past. Constance, from what you tell us, merits just a little thereof—then she may return', said Aramintha, sipping from her pink and white bone china cup.

'Aha! So you will warm her bottom! Good!', Jane laughed.

'I shall, indeed—and then...' She halted, dipped her spoon into the sugar bowl and nibbled the white grains.

'Shyness, you see', said Harry in the manner of a doctor pronouncing on a patient. 'What Aramintha meant to say, and which she has the will to say, but cannot bring herself to speak of it, is that Jenkins is better provided than are many men. Ten inches, that is, as she *chanced* to say. I have not measured it myself', he added hastily, 'but many is the lady whose natural needs he has had the girth and length to satisfy. Not in a lordly fashion—no, course that could not be the case, but with due deference, and always from the rear in order that the lady's lips are not besmirched by his. I have never known him kiss a female, dear, have you?', he asked his wife.

'Good heavens, Harry, no! That would be absolutely. . . . Positively, no! Mama knew a young valet once, quite handsome, too, but that was an otherness. You do not mind this conversation, dears, I hope?', she asked.

'At home we speak of it. Well—sometimes, just a little, yes', said Jane, whereat two pairs of eyes were quite a-sparkle. As to myself, I smiled in order to conceal the faint confusion that I felt.

'When one is civilised one does. How fearful are the houses where a total primness holds! As for myself, I have never come upon a cloud of golden *primnesses*', Harry remarked with a deft literary touch that I was pleased to recognise. I had thought myself as wandering just like Mr. Wordsworth's cloud before, but now felt more at ease.

'Jane wanted to see my husband's prick,' I said, and giggled suddenly, hand at my mouth.

'And did you, Jane? I say, what fun! My dears, let us not dissemble any more. Jenkins will service Constance after Aramintha has warmed her bottom up like toast. As for myself—dear Emily, I confess myself to have been entranced at the first sight of you. Constance will be sent back, her cunny bubbling with his sperm. May I then entertain you—yes?'

'Say yes!', begged Aramintha. I received a nudge from Jane upon the sofa where we sat.

'I shall be treated kindly in your hands—I have no doubt', I murmured, 'but as yet I have not, have not—well, I have not. . . .'

'Never, almost, or not quite?', asked Aramintha in surprise.

'All—if you want the truth', laughed Jane before I could summon up reply. 'I have both eyes and ears', she said on meeting my enquiring look.

'My dear. . . .', said Harry and all eyes turned to him. 'These young beauties must be a trifle tired from their exertions. May I suggest we deal with Constance on the morrow? To that purpose, Jenkins and I will visit in the morning. In that way, too, the wretched tribe will believe that Emily and Jane have reconsidered overnight and wish to make their peace'.

'Excellent, yes!', said Aramintha. She had a bright look in her eyes.

'Oh good! We can relax!', said Jane, whereat our hostess gave her a beguiling glance and said that she would show her to her room, while Harry could attend on me.

'Permit me, Emily', said Harry. He rose and offered me his arm. Aramintha beckoned Jane to her. I saw my sister use the same endearing, slouching step as she walked to the divan. Aramintha reached up and took her hand, Jane standing like a schoolgirl, looking down at her.

Over my shoulder, as I left the room on Harry's arm, I saw her sink down, and they tenderly embraced.

CHAPTER 10

The bed had black rails—bars, indeed—at either end. Surmounted on the corners were brass spheres that shone like four small suns. The coverlet was white, and fringed with pink: long tassels that might tickle me. Two heavy wardrobes brooded. In between them was a dressing table, busy with perfume phials and flasks of scented oil and pots of cream. Above the bed where the pillows became neighbours to the wall hung a black whip, its short and tapered tail curled like a serpent. A broad, tall mirror on a swivel-stand faced inwards to the bed from the far corner and reflected all.

The door closed, Harry took off his cravat and coat and placed them on a chair. I waited, licked my lips, and felt my mouth grow dry.

'Go to the corner—there, close to the mirror, head bowed, facing in, your dress pulled up. I wish to see your legs and bottom first', he said.

His words shocked me. I had expected first a tender kiss, the protestations of desire and admiration. I had already seen myself, face in his shoulder, being comforted.

'You mean to treat me badly, as the others did?', I asked, but did not turn my head to look at him.

'I mean to love you, Emily—hence you will show obedience. It is the only way with girls who have not been put to trials. I shall adore to suck upon your tongue, to lave your breasts with kisses, peck your nipples. Stiff will they rise, I have no doubt of it. You have a look of innocence and lewdness both, which well becomes you. Your sister Jane is similar, but has more boldness in the movements of her hips, as you must learn henceforth to have'.

'Oh! You mean I am to do it with anyone!'

'To the contrary, my pet, you will do it with whomever you wish—will say nay to several, will say yes to some, but first, with me, must learn submissiveness. Constance has tongued you, and you have seen her sister corked'.

'I have . . . I have . . . I have no need to learn', I muttered. How I longed for him to take me in his arms, and yet I felt before him as I used to with my tutor who would fondle my tits occasionally the while I blushed and read my broken Latin from a book, ignored his touch, but felt the swelling, proud.

'Go to the corner, Emily—obey!'

I slouched as Jane slouched, and felt mutinous—which was precisely what he intended me to feel. Head bowed, the dark flowers of the wallpaper underneath my eyes, I ruffled up my gown, exposed myself, my swelling globe, the offered cleft—was told to remain so, held my feet together and thus stood in an utter silence that he would not break.

I heard him casting off his clothes, boots falling with a clatter, heard the slithering of trousers, knew his nakedness unseen. The bed creaked, and I hunched my shoulders—waited, waited on commands. And yet in waiting I experienced precisely that which he intended me to do: the quivering sensation that a female knows when she offers up obedience to the male.

'Turn! Walk towards the bed—stand by the side of it—expose yourself', he uttered.

'Why do you make me do?', I whined, heard my own whine and felt ashamed of it. More so, perhaps, than showing him my bush, hairs fluffed, dark-brown upon my creamy skin. His penis, purplish at the knob, was full erect and wavered up his belly. Doubtfully, and showing doubtfulness in my slow steps, I moved until my stocking tops touched the bed's edge.

Placing his arms behind his head, his legs apart to show his balls, he asked me when I last was whipped.

I had not been, I said. He tutted, shook his head, and bid me hold my legs apart, yet the nature of his admonition showed amusement rather than dismay.

'You will pleasure penises tomorrow night the better for the instructions that I give you, Emily. Bend forward, place your palms upon the bed, and take my pego in your mouth, but do not touch it with your hands. No hesitations, dearest. Have you not sucked one before? It matters not—you have to learn the taste of it and feel the throb upon your tongue'.

I bent, but hesitated, wished to disobey. No sooner had I inclined my body with unwillingness than he reached and seized my hair, caused me to yelp, then urged the plum between my open lips and held my neck.

I gurgled, spluttered. O how meaty was his pulsing rod! Three inches, four, slid in upon my tongue, the swollen crest eased by my warm saliva. Inside myself I cried at the humiliation, as I thought of it, yet knew the hypocrisy of pleasure, too.

'More, Emily! Suck on it gently!' Up and down my head was bobbed by his impelling hand, the lewdness of the act repelling and enchanting me at the same time, mouth-moisture trickling down his tool which the more vibrant seemed the more I sucked. Then with such sweet brutality as made me gasp, he wrenched my mouth off, pulled me down upon him, falling sideways as I did, and took my mouth.

'Harry!', I sobbed.

'My darling, yes'.

My belly quivered, rippled, on his prick. My pussy hairs grazed at the root of it, my gown and my chemise dragged up by his quick hands to sting my nipples to his chest. He rolled me, rolled me then, until I lay beneath, eyes wide, my stockinged legs apart.

'D . . . d . . . d . . . do it to me, do!' I sobbed, my eyes, cheeks, corners of my mouth all kissed, he laughing, breathing heavily, one leg between my own, prick pulsing passionate against my stocking top.

'You will now be obedient, Emily?'

'Oh yes, I will!' My tongue intruded, whirled around his own, but he withdrew his mouth and knelt up, leaving me bereft, cock waggling stiffly to my view.

'Turn over, then, kneel up—your bottom thrust'.

'Not that way, Harry—no!', I whined, reached up my arms to draw him down, but squealed dismay as he then smacked my thighs.

'Turn OVER—bottom up!', he snapped, slapping my hips, I jerking this way, that. Tears started in my eyes. I looked dismayed, put on a woeful look, but had myself forced over and my bottom raised. Without preamble then he ringed my waist and hugged me into him and smacked my bared cheeks heftily, I squealing, 'No! Oh, Harry, don't!' Nape of my neck was held, nose buried in the pillow. Was I always to be handled so?

SMACK! SMACK!

'NEE-AAARGH! Please, don't—please don't!' My scorched cheeks wriggled to his blasting palm. I tightened them and pinched my nostrils, closed my eyes.

I was in purgatory, so I thought, instead of love's warm haven. Still, without remorse, he smacked my offered orb and brought the stinging deep until the flames licked inbetween.

'OH-WOH-WOH-WOH!', I sobbed and clenched my fists, pressing them through the pillow to the bolster's harder bulge beneath. I felt the heat irradiating through my cheeks and knew for the first time the sense of uttermost exposure and submission that it brings.

'*Remain*—or I will bring the whip to you', he said,

then slowly shuffled off the bed, I with face hid and squirming still, but did not dare to move. I heard a clink from near the dressing table, then Harry returned and knelt again behind me on the bed.—'Be still; I am anointing you', he said. I gasped, jerked, jittered as his finger, oiled, roamed carefully around my puckered hole and soothed warm lotion in. His hands then roughly spread my calves apart.

'A pity you were not attended to at home in this wise as most young girls are', I heard, then gritted out a squeak as the warm crest of his stiff penis—slippery in turn with oil—pushed in its helmet to invade my bottomhole.

'GAR! NO!', I sobbed. Both James and Constance, not to say her father, too, had slipped their fingers up me there, but this was bigger: the huge stave of flesh impelled itself relentlessly within until I felt my breath expelled, clawed at the pillow and beseeched his grace or mercy, or whatever word came quite haphazard to my lips.

'Obedience, Emily!', he growled.

Ah, that our language—richer surely than are most—had more élan, more glitter (call it what you will) when lending itself to descriptions of the acts of love! I was being sodomised, was being buggered, and how wretchedly rough and aggressive are those words— how crude their connotations, and how harsh they sound! Better to say that I was being pistoned, for I have heard it since called such, or being 'corked' which, at the least, has a greater homeliness to it. Many are the maidens I have seen, long since, having their derrieres plugged, and none emerged from it with tears, though often breathless, having spent the while the penis moved within their nether holes.

One panics at the first. The pity of it, but one does, unless long fingering and sweet caresses first have done their work and charmed the girl to offer it, hardnippled, langourous, as she becomes. One wriggles, but that aids one's conqueror. As for myself, I reached my hands up, gripped the bed's iron rail and pushed back pettishly, the movement serving only to embed his corker deeper.

'NOO-HOO! NOO-HOO!', I petulantly sobbed. A strangled 'AH!' escaped me as he thrust my head and shoulders roughly down, forced me to loose my hold, then rooted in until his balls nubbed underneath my nest.

'Ah, Emily, what a fine plump arse you have!', growled Harry. Pulsing in my yielded hole, which so expanded magically and clenched his tool in a warm, spongy grip, he moved his poker gently back and forth, creating such sensations that I all but swooned, felt my head feathery and light, my bottom bigger, bulging to his flesh. I jerked and quivered, hips clasped by his palms, yet dared not move too much. The stinging that I first had felt began to fade. I felt my clitoris a-tingle, then his right hand cupped my hairy notch and soothed it gently, causing me to squirm in such a manner as delighted him. Drawing his throbbing shaft half out, he held it thus and fingered round my spot.

'There, darling, there. You have your first prick up your bottom. Contain it, squeeze upon it, roll your hips but gently and not overmuch'.

'Oh, Harry!' Yet my wail was not then of despair. I felt it slip in, out, my passage eased by Nature's lubrications. Snorting softly, I permitted him to part the oily lips of my plump quim and felt emergent tremors of delight. I moaned, I whimpered, but I could not speak. Huge clouds of cobwebbed words were in my mind. I could not speak. Rude words, obscene words, danced within the hollows of my mind. Papa had cupped my bottom, kissed my lips. I know the purpose of his asking me if I had learned to kiss. It was to become a secret password in my life.

86

'I am withdrawing it, my love. Be still, and then turn over when I do. Lie with your arms extended in a cross, your legs apart and knees drawn up'.

'Ooooh!', I uttered as his long, thick piston then withdrew. It hesitated at the rim, held there—the knob just bulging in me—then slipped out—left me forlornly empty, to my great surprise. Laggard in turning, I obeyed. The ring of my probed rose felt open still. My bottom smarted on the coverlet, he looming over me, descending till his penis brushed my belly and then nosed my curls. His hands fell on my wrists—extended as they were—and held them down. I had almost come already and was nigh to doing so as the proud crest parted my lovelips in two rippling waves, causing my back to arch, whereat he plumped his full weight down on me, mouthed lips to mine and eased his penis slowly in my nest.

'Your stockings and your garters feel delicious, Emily. Rub them against my thighs. You beauty! I adore to fuck a girl half dressed'.

I heard but dimly, all my being concentrated on the insurgence of his cock within my quim. I rolled my bottom, moaned, received four inches, five—and ever on. Clawing his back, my trembling knees apart, I laboured his tongue wetly with my own and sobbed increasing pleasure. *Fuck*. I had never heard the word before. It came with harshness to my ears, and has a roughness I have never liked. Better to be 'threaded', 'nested-in', or even 'poked'. Yet even so, the word has a crude magic of its own that I admit to having given way to sometimes in the thrall of it.

'Ask me to fuck you, Emily!'

He held me still, arms straight, wrists gripped, as though I might not surrender to love's toil. Then he released his hold and cupped my bottom with both hands, raising it from the counterpane and ramming full within so suddenly that the soft SMACK! of our loins sounded.

'HAAAR!', I gasped. My head hung back, mouth slipping upwards and away from his. His face, no longer handsome, was demonic. I was mastered, pinned. Faint liquid sounds came from my cunny as he worked his piston back and forth.

'Fuck, yes!', I spluttered, 'fuck me, Harry, do!'

'Whisper it, my love, against my lips'.

I whispered, whispered ever on, and counted not the times I said the words, abandoned as I felt. My cunny bubbled, spurted, spilled, salivas mingling and my arms about his neck, my bottom swinging, cradled on his palms. The bed squeaked its delight beneath my form, breath panting, nose to nose and mouth to mouth, his pulsing penis grooving in and out.

'I am coming! Oh, my love, too soon! Forgive me, but your beauty—AAARGH!'

'Oh, Harry, yes!'

I felt the first thick, gruelly spurt—the next—another then, his penis ticking madly as he spewed love's juice between my spongy walls, and I in a pale blur of wonderment, pursued by howling devils of delight, came in my turn again and thus anointed him, though his sweet agony was clearly such that I doubt he felt my thinner drops.

Expending then, expending the last pearls, the final squirt of juice, then we collapsed, I hugging his thick corker in my dell and squeezing on it lovingly. Long thus we stayed, his balls squashed up to me, my bottom heavy on his resting palms that dug into the sheet beneath.

'You have known all now, Emily—or almost all— the fond delights of it', he uttered, drawing out the shrinking slug of his much softened pleasure-rod.

'Yes', I murmured, felt both shy yet bold at the same time and made to close my legs but was affectionately smacked to leave them open to his view, he lying then beside me with my face into his neck, my belly rippling in the aftermath, my cuntlips pouting, frothed with sperm and my own spendings.

'Tomorrow night there will be more than one who will seek to take his place between your legs. You may say nay to one, but not to both. You understand?'

'Yes, Harry'.

Inbetween my sighs we kissed. Softly we kissed— raindrops of kisses on my parted lips, my dress all bundled up above my breasts whose tingling nipples told their own tale of delight. He would not have me silent, though, for long, and brought me to confess all that I knew, had heard, had done. Even to Jane, and Julie, too.

'Your cousin, then, imbibed the manly juice between her lips? And Jane was trestled? Yes, I understand how that was done, for Aramintha does the same trick with some girls, and then I perforate their bottoms while they squeal. Though not for long they squeal. No more than you, my pet', he laughed, and I a-blushing, saying that it was not true of me—or would not be in future.

'Is it not cruel to whip?', I asked, and glanced up at the one that hung above, remembering how my father-in-law had scourged my globe, though in retrospect it had not hurt that much.

'It is not cruel, my love, to spur a maiden to surrender if she proves too coy to drop her drawers upon command. A girl should be nurtured at an early age, and given pride in both her muff and her bottom cheeks. The whip induces—is not meant to torture her. Heaven forfend it should! The cane is more admonitory. As to birches, when the twigs are softened they but make the bottom wriggle and the ardour rise. The girl's cheeks feel fuller; she is ready to receive. Frequently the parental penis is inserted first—but not in your case'.

'Not in mine, no. Harry, you were first. You surely know you were'.

'Indeed—and that I treasure, Emily. Aramintha has no jealousy when two are tingling, cock to cunt. You may think it strange, but such is so'.

'I do not think it strange. The pleasure is divine and all should share it, should they not?', I asked naively.

'You wait upon my affirmation even though you have it in your heart? All who have lustiness upon them should resolve their hot desires and do so with such eagerness as makes their bodies melt for it. Feel no remorse for consummations that are mutually sought, fulfilled. Be as a bird that flies and roosts, and flies again, and questions not the sky, nor trees nor earth'.

'Yes, Harry; that I always wished to be, and now...'

'Harry, have you not finished yet with the dear girl? Do not exhaust her. It is time to eat!', came Aramintha's voice from down below, I starting up, but Harry bid me take my time, repair my hair and look my best.

'Do I not always?', I riposted. Now that it was over I felt flirtatious, eager for the next. He, answering cheerfully, 'Beyond all doubt!', we made ourselves respectable and ventured down to find Jane buttoning up her dress.

'Was it nice? Was nice, yes? Was it nice?', asked Aramintha, tilted up my chin and kissed my lips.

I said, 'Yes, oh it was!', as if we had but picnicked, gathered flowers, or paddled in a stream.

Jane said, 'Oh, Emily, do up my top button, please— I cannot reach it'. And with that, a warm enclave of homeliness enfolded all my sins.

CHAPTER 11

That night, Jane and I—sleeping together as Aramintha suggested we might in order to discuss our future plans—fell to much lip-chewing talk of what to tell Mama and Papa.

'No doubt they have already heard from those frightful people who are now your in-laws', Jane opined.

'I think not, no. They will wait until at least later tomorrow, expecting me to have a change of mind—and that will certainly not occur. We will send a message in the morning to say that we are well, and staying with good friends'.

'Then Papa will come and have a quarrel, I am sure of that'.

'If you think such, you do not know him well. Let us ask for Julie to call on us. In that way, Papa will have news without a public confrontation that he would not seek', I said. And so it was arranged. Jenkins took a maid by horse and cart first thing, for I thought it best that a servant, young and of good appearance (I saw myself to it that she was well spruced-up) should present herself rather than an awkward, burly male.

'Such polish for your age!', Aramintha complimented me.

'I do not want Constance to be polished, though. Much as I would like to see it done, it would not amuse me and, besides, she might go hollering to the world outside', I said.

'True, true', said Harry, who appraised me differently at that. Even so, I looked upon his treatment of me with a pleasure that surprised, and came to a better understanding of how young ladies feel when they are disciplined in order to first take the cock. In the discreet way of the pair, however, nought was said of it. I was allowed to return to that state of apparent demureness and sweet innocence that I had always worn, though underneath my skirt was a warm readiness for more.

The household contained but three servants: a cook, a maid, and Jenkins. More were an encumbrance, Aramintha said, and not in an excusing way, for she explained that when her discreet parties were held, it were best that a wandering servant did not interrupt the revelries.

'Your gardens will be watered. Are you well prepared for that?', she asked us in her sometimes languid way.

I meant not to be second in reply, and said immediately I was, and so was Jane—and this before my sister spoke. It prided me to turn the tables on her just a little.

'Who shall there be?' I asked.

'Ah! Wait and see! Names have no meaning. All are utterly conversant with our rules—which is to say that a young lady can be persuaded but not forced. There are initiations sometimes, but tonight there will not be . . . alas!', our hostess uttered with a laugh.

'The last one—several months ago—was a very, an exceedingly, sweet sixteen', Harry said, and said it in such manner that I knew he was inviting us to ask.

'Oh? Was she tasted first?', I asked boldly, whereat Aramintha clapped her hands and said she was delighted to know I had such knowledge.

'Lucinda is her name', said Harry, and went on, 'You would have adored her, both of you, for she looked demure, and really was. We treated her with utmost gentleness, you understand. An uncle of hers brought her, he being the appointed one to see her made fit and ready for the sport. I doubt that she had ever seen a penis in erection, though had had her bottom fondled, but no more'.

'Aha, she had not learned to kiss', I said.

'Precisely, Emily. Or not, at least, with open mouth and searching hands. The first hour was a warming-up of drinks and laughter. Pleasantries were said — not rude but quite suggestive. Lucinda was wide-eyed, remained against the wall, a flush upon her cheeks. She had not known such company before, free-speaking, merry, and yet civilised. Her glass was filled again, again.'

'Oh, that was not fair!', said Jane, and Aramintha raised her eyebrows high.

'It was merely to make her *vibrant*, darling. One cannot expect a virgin to be taken if her veins do not throb a little at the least. I dearly wished to kiss her first, and did. The lights were lowered; the room almost dark. Ladies and gentlemen began to dance, and I pressed Lucinda up against the wall — from which she had scarcely moved in any case — and pressed my lips to hers. Oh, what a darling mouth she had! Sweet was the nectar that I drew from it. She was too timid to resist, and was also — if I dare to say so — warm for an embrace. My hands up to her cheeks, and she blinded in the fond embrace, my sister, Ambrosia, approached, sandwiched her between us and took her mouth in turn until I am sure Lucinda knew not where she was.

'At that', Aramintha continued, 'Harry turned up the lamps, and between us Lucinda was blindfolded and held. I thought it best — solicitous, you know. She cried out and tried to drag back, but we brought her to the centre of the room, then quickly upped her skirt and got her white drawers off'.

'After a struggle. What a noise she made!', laughed Harry.

'Well, of *course* she did, and so would I have done, my dear. The shock of it! But that was soon allayed. My sister held Lucinda's wrists behind her back while

93

I kneeling, forced my face up inbetween her thighs and set to licking at her cunny slit. The little devil bumped and squirmed. There was no mocking laughter, though. Such is not done. The whole affair was carried out in silence. Chubby as her bottom was, I held it clasped in both my palms and brought her clitoris to tingle up'.

'Which made her moan, I bet', said Jane, her eyes as bright as mine, cheeks flushed.

'Darling, she *really* moaned. I was a full three min-utes—more, perhaps—a-licking at her honeypot until she spilled, and then her knees sagged and her head hung back, although she whimpered still, 'Oh, don't!' Fortunate it is that we females spend much more than men! I rose; another lady set to work on her. Again Lucinda bucked and twisted, but more in pleasure than in dire embarrassment. My sister twisted then Lucinda's neck and brought her mouth once more to hers. Much spluttering was heard, but finally the girl succumbed. Her knees sagged once again—once more she came'.

'Oho, it was much more than a simple tasting then', said Jane.'

'You *know* then? Have you been . . . Oh well, it does not matter. If you have not, you are past that point. Some use the birch while others use their tongues', our hostess said, and then continued, '*Actually*, my dears, this was intended to be rather more than just a tasting. Lucinda was to be enflamed beyond mere titillations and was due back in her bed at midnight, ready for the cock'.

'Go on!', I interrupted, for I could not wait to hear the end after my own escape that morn. If such it was. I wondered if it was, and if I might not afterwards have slipped into my bed and had no more of Arnold from that moment on.

'I am, my pet!', laughed Aramintha in surprise. 'The men, as you can well imagine, were by then in a very upright state. Lucinda's quim was tight and luscious, sprinkled with the prettiest of curls. Her thighs were fresh young columns, girded by grey stockings and with garters black. Quite saucy, though she had not thought it so when she had dressed demurely in her room, I'm sure. Her chemise was lovely—pink, and frilled with white, with little bows a-dancing round the hem. We tucked it up, well up, to bare her navel and her bottom for the fray, then she was carried bleating to a table where a cushion had been placed to keep her tummy warm. Hung over it, and both arms held by Ambrosia and myself, her toes just touched the floor, but not enough to dig and push. Such details are important, doncherknow!'

'Her uncle, then', said Harry, but was interrupted smartly by his wife.

'Shush, dearest, I am telling this! Her uncle, yes, of course. The rogue was eager for the fray and bared his prick. She was only to be 'dipped', though, and he had to show constraint, as did the others here. While Lucinda cried and swirled her stockinged legs about, he approached her stealthily and seized her hips in a strong clasp to keep her chubby bottom still. Oh dear, oh dear—how she cried out! The blindfold was still around her eyes, of course. His trousers sagged and then he bent his knees and brought his swollen crest up to her honey-lips.

'She screeched at the first touch of it! I waggled my free hand at him to have a care. His rubicund expression, mouth agape at the first touch of his niece's cunny to his cock, inflamed him much, of course. I knew he must not ram her full, nor spill. That was not to be the game at all. So over-eager did he look! Oh, Harry, yes, you need not glare. All men do at such times— why, even you! A long-pitched cry from dear Lucinda and his cock urged up her creamy channel, first an inch, then two, then three—at which I waved my hand at him again!

95

'He had to grit his teeth and hold her thus, just one-third sheathed, poor devil, but there was no help for it. Lucinda was intended just to know the feel of it. His thighs were all a-tremble, you can guess! His eyes beseeched mine, but I shook my head and counted silently, albeit with lips that he could see and read, to two score, then with dulling eyes he drew it out of her tight nest and another—to a howl from her—succeeded in his place'.

'How many were there?', Jane asked, open-mouthed, and nudged me as she spoke as though I had been accomplice to the act or had seen such before.

'How many? Five, my dear! The ladies waited in their readiness to have the best of it, discarding dresses, drawers, their pussies pouting and expectant. Lucinda's uncle mounted one of them upon some cushions on the floor. The two writhed in the uttermost delight and watched Lucinda take her second offering. She mewed and tried to wriggle off the cock, but was well-held. Alas, the warmth of both her clefts was too much for the gentleman, and with an expression of agony and lust, he withdrew his steaming piston only halfway through my two-score count and spattered her wriggling bottom with his jets of sperm, the which—oddly— seemed to mollify her, for she ceased to cry out loud and set to whimpering in that silly way a young girl does when she discovers in herself a liking for a certain naughtiness.

'The sperm was trickling down her ivory bottom cheeks when the third gentleman raised her hips the more, and clamped her well, and entered in. He was her champion; had done the trick before, and with the greatest effort kept his prick a-throb in her—half in, no more—for a full count of fifty before he turned back to his dear wife who received him with parted lips and open legs and much affection, as you well may guess.

'At the entry of the fourth and fifth, Lucinda was

much less dismayed. A lewd observer might have said that her cunnylips by then were ridged with hot desire, but as for myself I noted that she uttered only a soft "Oooh-Wer!" as each let her feel his poker burn within her grotto. Naturally, both Ambrosia and myself comforted her much with whispers all the time and bid her push her bottom out, said naughty words to her and even asked her if she was obtaining pleasure from the cocks. Of course, she only bleated in reply'.

'A young girl's role is almost always one of nearly silent pleasure', Harry said.

'And well you should know, dear, but they often moan delightfully', his wife said. Then she carried on, 'The ladies being occupied, we carried a limp Lucinda up the stairs, untied her blindfold and caressed and kissed her on the bed. "Why did you—why?", she whimpered, but could not resist. Her drawers were kept as a souvenir. I think, though, that by then she had almost forgotten she had ever had them on. We cozened her and told her that the night would be more pleasant for her than she had ever known. I must say that the dear child was in a loving daze by then and clung to me and Ambrosia and asked us not to take her down again. This being assured, she tidied up herself. I took her wine and biscuits and she sat with my dear sister for an hour until all the revelries were done below.

'In the way of things, the guests were ushered out— they wishing not to cause the sweet girl any more embarrassment. Only her uncle remained and looked his solemn best. She blushed muchly when we took her down to him, but without a word save of praise for her appearance, he offered up his arm and led her out to the waiting carriage, I accompanying them with much bright chatter of quite ordinary things.

'Oh, how discreet you are!', I uttered.

'My dear, one *must* be. Had she been threaded already, then it would have been quite other. We have had girls here little past her age who take the cock with pleasure, absolutely blind to those who see them in their naughtiness. Bonviviality breeds a daring that does not come otherwise, and with punch in their tummies they are ready to be tickled up, especially when their elders show the way.'

'Have you seen her since, and will she come again?', Jane asked.

'I think not for several months at least. She is being kept in purdah, as it were, which will not harm her. It is not wished that she should indulge herself too much with others yet, and that is wise. Girls of her age who become too libertine lose any air of mystery they might have had. She has learned a little lewdness, is submissive, has had her bottom plugged, her cunny, too', said Aramintha with some satisfaction.

'Why did you ask?', I asked Jane afterwards.

'I just wondered, that was all. I wondered what it felt like'.

'Huh! You already know', said I.

'I don't mean *that*. I told you I was trestled, had my bottom corked, but I was not blindfolded, or anything like that. And no one else was there. I mean . . .'

'Why, really, you are almost jealous, Jane!', I laughed.

'Not really, no. I just wondered . . . Well . . . it must be awful fun to have—well, *you* know—five things, cocks, and not to know whose they may be. And then to be nicely comforted afterwards', she added a little mournfully.

'I suppose the whip stung you, and you were not comforted—and that's the truth of it', I said.

'It did, of course, it did! He was quite adamant to make me take my drawers down—show myself. I knew I had to, though. One does'.

'One does', I echoed. Papa had made me pull my drawers up when he might well have birched my own.

I knew I would have submitted to that, too, and felt a flush rise in my cheeks.

'What are you thinking of?', asked Jane, and no doubt cogitated that I thought of her. I pretended that I did, to flatter her. I thought, though, of a myriad things: of drawers pulled down, of drawers pulled up, and toying with my cunny at stray thoughts of naughtiness, and semen shooting up the virile stems, late nights when I had waited to be kissed and no one came, the days of childhood put away, and my thighs warm.

But was that all I thought, or cared for now? The richnesses of pleasure are truly infinite. On nibbling small, iced cakes and drinking tea, one knows a sensuous pleasure, even as one does in choosing a new gown—but more, yes more (I knew that I was truly drawn to it), the pleasures of a penis pumping in one's honeypot, or unforgiving inbetween one's bottom cheeks.

'Jane, if you did not *truly* like someone, but were in the dark—had not much on—would you then let him do it to you, if he tried?'

'I would with my bottom up; I would not need to look! That's why, you silly, I wondered what it's like to have a blindfold round your eyes. Just as a game, I mean', she added, and her eyes were warm: a small fire waiting for the fires that would be lit in winter yet.

CHAPTER 12

Our baggage was returned.

Harry came back with Jenkins, and the servant brought it up. He entered first my room and gazed at me with awe as though I might be a Princess in The Tower.

'We got 'em all, Miss. Bit of a fuss there was, but they stayed back. The master, he wouldn't have no truck with nonsense—nor would I'.

'I am so grateful, Jenkins. Bring them in, please do. I cannot lift them, or I would myself.'

'You don't have to do that, Miss. It's what I'm here for, humping, carrying, and helping out. I don't grumble at it, though. It's a good life. Good beer, good vittals. There is many as does not have those'.

'Is that your whole life, Jenkins? Is there nothing more that you desire?'

'Miss, there are many things a man desires, but dares not speak of them. When I was younger, I was put to ladies by the score—led in like a prize bull and did my deed, my service as I calls it. Well enough they praised me'.

'I am sure they did'. I felt myself upon the point of indiscretion and made room for him as he hauled the trunks within. A nervous itching was within me that I could not properly control, yet I was out of place with this rough man—wanted to die from him, not yet. I wished myself a calmness that I did not have. Ten inches, Aramintha had proclaimed. I wondered nervously and naughtily as to the truth of that, and tried to turn my thoughts to otherness, but Jenkins seemed to sense my wondering, and hovered as he brought the last bag in. I turned my back, clasped my hands and brought my knuckles to my mouth like a child eager to open a parcel, and yet too excited to.

'I know what you're thinking, Miss, if I may make so bold. I seen it happen often. There's no harm to it. I wouldn't assault your person if you did not want. As to my freedom in respect of such, Miss Aramintha lets me have it full'.

The last sentence, coming so quaintly to my ears, brought me to giggle, whereat I also blushed and dropped my head, still biting on my knuckles as I did.

'Does she?' I forced the words out, but I could not turn. He stepped away from me. I heard the key turn in the lock and would have screamed, and would have screamed, but held my tongue and—yes—my breath as well.

'You be nice and quiet, Miss—that's the best', I heard.

I gasped out a little 'Oh!' and felt his large hands on my shoulders.

'Do not!', I gritted, hunched my shoulders, but he held them still.

'You has to move away, Miss, if you will not— that's the rule. A good one as it is. It gives consent without the words, you see. Tell you a good few stories, that I could, about such things.'

'I don't know what you mean', I burbled, but I did not move. His hands slid slowly down my back, curved underneath my bottom, and he held me there— my 'plum' again upon two lordly palms. Surely he would not ask me, dare not ask, if I had learned to kiss?—'J... J... J... J... !', I stammered, for his hands were carefully drawing up my skirt, calves bared, and then my knees, and then my stocking tops.

'Handsome legs you got, Miss—boo-tiful! Let's see your bum now. Don't be frit of words. My goodness, what a peach—a split peach, as I bin taught to call it, and it's true. I seen yours wobble as you walk, not fat but tight. Round as the moon, it is'.

'I w... won't let you, Jenkins!'—but my little cry dissolved in air as soon as it was spoke. I had not moved an inch. My toes were curled inside my shoes, my eyes half closed, his palms a-soothing round my bared, plump cheeks.

'OOOH!' came from me. He drew the cheeks apart and held me swaying, teetering.

'I can be rough or tender with you, Miss. Now that you've let me bare your bum. That is the rule of it, in this house and in others that I've bin. Some ladies like it rough, they do, but others not. Now roll your cheeks, Miss, on my palms. Lean back agin me—come up on tiptoe'.

'I can't!', I wailed. A small, thin wail that never would have escaped the door.

'Papa had said 'on tiptoe'—he had.

'I got a fair belt on, Miss. I can bring it to your arse, if that you want. Some girls prefer it. Both my daughters do'.

I turned, I did not mean to turn. I needed comforting, as Jane had said she needed or preferred. My hot face pressed into his shoulder—blind my eyes.

Tilting, my hands perched like two sparrows on his brawny shoulders, I came up on tiptoe while he cupped my arse again. It was a rare word to me then, and yet I used it to myself. More blatantly than I thought I could, I moved the silky bulb upon his palms.

'You haven't really, Jenkins? Do they? Do they really do?'

'As soon as they were ripe, Miss, yes. I scorched their bottoms several times, and then they saw the stand I had on me, a cockstand that I mean, and I saw that they saw.'

'Just tell me, Jenkins. Talk to me'.

'Ah, you likes a bit of naughty talk! Well, many do.

I'm up to it myself; it stirs the senses really well. Bertha—she were seventeen—and Mary was younger by two years. They used to roll their bottoms when I strapped them—sobbed they did, but never really howled. Their mother always told them to be quiet, you see, and when they were I give 'em only a dozen, not a score such as they often needed, traipsing all about and being idle, kicking up a dust about their shoes and frocks. A man like me, Miss, don't have the coins to spend on such. Don't squeeze your bumcheeks, Miss, too tight. Just let me get my finger in'.

'Ooooh, Jenkins!'

The thick tip of his digit in my rose. It moved around the puckered rim, then slipped quite delicately in. I absorbed an inch of it, then it was still.

'What did they say, do, Jenkins, when you d...d ...d...did this?'

'It's the first surprise of it that catches them. You straps them, gets their bottoms hot, then whirls them round upright and corks them with your fingertip. Beat at me first with her fists did Bertha until I growled at her and told her as she yet might have another dose. Did all her sobbing then, she did. I held her corked like this, Miss, then I lifted her chemise and felt her titties. Nice and round they were, the nipples up and sparky from the strap. First time I gives her just a kiss or two and eased my finger in and out, but not enough to startle her too much. Her knees sagged, and I knew she had the feel of it.'

'It makes me d...d...dizzy, Jenkins!'

'Course it does—and holds you helpless, don't it, all a-stirring in your belly. Yes, I knows the way of it all right. She felt my cock, as you can, through my clothes. Fair frantically it ticked, but then I eased my finger out and told her to get dressed. I was in a rare state, that I tell you, so was she. Her face was flushed. I saw her eagerness'.

'And then you did it to her?'

'No, Miss, no. I knew she'd be expectant more, the next time that the leather scorched her cheeks. I told my wife, and asked her what to do. You'd better let me kiss you, Miss. I likes to feel the tongues of girls when they're coming up on heat'.

'I can't, no, Jenkins!'

Even as I spoke, I roamed my hand down to his great projection, felt its enormous length and girth beneath his trouser cloth, and allowed my lips to come beneath his own. Timid my tongue. He growled into my mouth, snapped my head back and sought it, sucked it in, making me so swoony that he had to hold me up by invading my bottomhole a little more. I sobbed with pleasure and he liked the sound.

'Martha, she said to me, "You give it to the girl, if that she needs. Farm boys will cover her, if you don't first". I took her word for it and had the girl upstairs that night. Real coy she were. She knew what she were in for. "No, I won't", she says, and sets to giggling when I got her dress off, but I saw she had a fresh chemise on, so expected it. I had to lambast her first, Miss, and she knew I did'.

My eyes were rolling up into my head. My bottomhole was open to his finger's probe, felt hot and spongy, ready to receive.

'Oh, Jenkins, take me on the bed!'

'I will that, Miss. Now, lie upon the bed, your legs apart. I likes to see 'em thus, bush boldly shown and belly nice and flat and thighs held wide'.

'Oooh!' His finger had uncorked itself. He urged me gently back and let me fall, stripped off his jacket as I swung my legs and lay obedient, one arm across my eyes, though—peeping—I could see his trousers coming down and saw the hugeness of him, stark and bold, emerging. Thick as a stave it was and quite as long as Aramintha had declared, the crest enormous, glowing purplish-pink. But 'OW!' I uttered then, for as he neared the bed, he smacked my nearest leg and bid me draw my knees up.

'You be quiet, Miss. Keep your arm across your eyes and when I tries to take it off, don't let me do. You understand?'

'Yes!', I quavered, heard him lift his shirt, then felt his hairy belly come on mine. His knob grazed in my cunthairs, then descended slowly to the waiting lips whose puffiness and moisture brought a pleased grunt from his throat. I wanted to cry out—compressed my lips—and held my forearm tightly across my eyes. A little 'Oh!' escaped me as the plum parted the convoluted waves of flesh and urged within the bubbling of my dell. The helmet seemed to split me, and I bucked.

'No, Miss, I got to hold you down', he growled. His elbows pressed against my inner thighs, hands grasped the curving of my hips.

'Don't—don't!', I moaned, but even so I lifted up my bottom as I spoke, the better to present myself to him, whereat he tried to draw my arm away, but I resisted, whimpered.

'Just like Bertha were', he said, and at that I could not help myself but threw my arms around his neck and strained and strained to slowly draw him in.

'She let you fuck her. Oh, you naughty man!', I mouthed.

'A real good fuck she is, Miss, too. Yes, even now— she's married but comes back to have a lathering from her Dad's cock. It fills her like no other does, as it do yours'.

'Goo-goo! Oh, it's too big! No! Oh yes!'

My god, what a delirium! All thoughts of wickedness, desire and love embraced me all at once. The man's huge penis was embedded inch by inch. The apples of his balls (I cannot call them less) bulged up beneath my bottom. Ah, what ecstasies of thoughts, sensations, entrance one in such moments! I moaned, I clawed at him, said words I never thought to speak, had visions that I never thought to have. The walls of my honeypot expanded to his stave most wondrously and gripped the throbbing veins.

'I got yer as I wanted to! From the first moment that I saw you, Miss, I meant to get between your legs'.

'Did you? Oh tell me, do I then feel nice?'

'More luscious than I ever had. Better by far you are than all of 'em. You wants to feel me spunk in you?'

Spunk? I had never heard the word before, but in my wild excitement knew what it must mean.

'Spunk me, sperm me, if you want to, yes', I moaned. His shaft was oily with my exudations. Hissing breath against each other's nostrils we began to thresh. Each drawing out and plunging in of his huge corker was sheer ecstasy.

'Not yet, Miss. I likes to bring you on. A girl has to have her pleasure first, or won't come back before. When Bertha come, she squealed and bit my shoulder, then I squirted her. All right now, wrap your legs up over mine and work yer lovely arse to it. I'll hold it for you—swing it back and forth'.

'Yes, yes, come on. Do it, do it—I don't care what you do! Ah, Jenkins, what a prick you have!'

'Don't call me that, Miss. Call me Dad, or darling, dear, and put your tongue in as you talk. Ah, little devil, you are coming, I can feel!'

'D...d...d...Dad, oh darling, dear!', I stammered quite berserk and spilled and spilled, my belly tightening and relaxing with each squirt, my tongue a-lashing in his mouth. Torrents of lust. I felt no other then. Lust was the devil that drew up one's skirts and pinned one down and rode one in a torment of delight, knowing no other than the thrill of it. —'Come in me, come!', I blethered, clawed his back and knotted up my legs around his waist and jerked and gasped.

'You wait for it, you little bitch!'

'Oh-woh!', I moaned. He had the power to keep me pinned beneath him all the day if he so wished, moving his heavy loins back-forth, rubbing his bristly pubic hairs to mine, balls slapping. —'Oooh! Your balls!', I gasped, and knew myself to be a thousand women all at once, the high, the low, submissive, ardent underneath the mastering weight of him, the purposeful, deep surging of his cock.

'Say that you want my cock', he growled.

'I want, I want, I want!', I sobbed and heard him utter a deep 'AAH!', his oily helmet all but slipping out. And then he poised himself, so poised, and held me in attendant agony, seizing my face and making me upstare into his burning eyes. For one long moment so we stared. I knew the mystery of that anguished stare, the moment frozen as if we had ever been thus, cock to cunt, the hot deliberation of the moment held.

'Say yes!'

His strange insistence was a spell on me, I rimming with my tightened lovelips his stilled helmet, pulsing as it was.

'Har, yes! Oh Dad, oh darling, dear, oh yes! F... f... fuck me, do it in me, do!'

'Good girl! You knows to do it now, all right. Now you remember that and how it's done. Right up you now, my little pet, and take it all!'

'WAH-HAH!' I sobbed. He came down on me flat again, tongue to my tongue and urged himself up in. He groaned, he jerked, he held it for a moment longer while I clenched my velvet walls around his conqueror and pouted up my lips to him in such wise as I knew I must, seeping my warm breath in his mouth as with insensate gasps he loosed his first jet. The thick porridge spattered, swirled and pelleted with ardent force and caused my walls to palpitate around his tool.

'C... coming in you like I said I would', he moaned.

'Yes, yes! Oh, do it more! Oh, lovely, yes!'

His jets, so powerful, made a foaming flood that wet the coverlet beneath. I spent again, I sobbed, repeating all the wild obscenities he flooded at the same time in my ear—repeated them by rote, yet knew the tang of them, knew them as salt and pepper to the feast.

'GRRR!', came his grunt. Embedded in my spermy channel full, he came and quivered, came again, then sank down on my breast. My drumming heels scraped at his buttocks, then we sighed a huge deep sigh, were still, the thick cock of him pulsing and expending pearly raindrops of delight.

'You'll lie still now and keep your legs apart as I get up'.

And I said 'Yes', I said, said 'Yes'.

The cork drew slowly out. I let my legs relax, let them slip down and held them wide. The weeping crest of him kissed both my lovelips, rubbed around my spot and made me quiver, then he rose.

'I filled you up, Miss, that I did'.

The bed sagged and sprang up again as he got off and looked down at my thick, cream-spattered bush.

I did not answer, did not know the words to say. Splayed open, so I waited while he drew his trousers up and gathered up his jacket from a chair.

'Best to be silent for the moment, Miss. It shows consent, you see, to what we done. Keeping your legs apart says 'Yes'. I taught my Bertha that, and Mary, too. You've learned from what I've taught you, and I know you have.'

I threw my arms once more across my eyes to hide the sight of him, said 'Yes'. I knew that he expected it.

'Keep all your learning, Miss, inside your head. Some gents, they likes you to be shy, while others don't. Best to be shy if you ain't sure. Struggle a bit, you can, but not too much. Wait till the knob is in, that's what I always say. Wriggle your bottom, be tempestuous. It always brings the passion up. I'll let you tidy up yourself, Miss, now'.

Then he was gone, the door unlocked again. I closed my thighs, then opened them, and giggled tightly up against my hand.

'I care not who does it to me now', I thought.

And knew it almost to be true.

CHAPTER 13

Harry knew, and Aramintha knew—I swear they did. Their looks were faintly searching when I ventured down. Jane was in the garden gathering flowers, and had been there a long time, so I hoped.

'Did Jenkins see to you? He brought it up to you?', asked Harry with a grin.

'What did they say? Did you see Arnold? Who was there?', I countered, and admired myself for that. I had doused my face with water and my cheeks were no longer flushed. My hairpins were exactly placed, my dress was smooth. My cunny felt deliciously plump. Its lips were silent, and they could not make them speak.

'A vulgar woman spoke to me. One by the name of Hilda, I believe. The husband lurked and was not seen. Her husband, Emily; I saw not yours. A girl appeared—the younger one whom you described. She asked if you were well'.

'She asked? Asked that?' I felt surprise, and such small and unnecessary guilt as brushes like a cobweb to the mind.

'She had a soft look in her eyes. I thought it sincere—maybe it was not. The deuce of it, all females act so well when called upon to do so by a circumstance they wish to change. As to the mother, she said they disowned you—having nothing else to say—for I made it plain I knew more than I hinted at'.

'Clever Harry—always tactful, always strong', said Aramintha with affection, though rather challenging me to speak of something else, I felt.

'I am so grateful to you, Harry. Yes, when Jenkins

brought my bags up, he looked at me most strangely, in a quite possessive way. I scarce knew how to speak to him, but was polite, of course'.

'Of course you were, my dear. That is the measure of our class', said Aramintha, screwing up her brow a little and yet—as I saw—believing me.

'He is an old retainer, then?', I asked.

'Oh, on and off', she answered oddly, and then Jane came in, blooms flourished, and the subject turned towards the evening. The revels would begin at eight o'clock, we learned. Dinner would be served early and all cleared away before the guests arrived. As to myself, my mind was busy with the message I had sent to Papa and Mama, how they would take to it, and what might come to be. I had no fear of it but rather a cool curiosity that was dissolved just after lunch when Julie was announced.

'Oh, denizen from another world!', I laughed in my relief, and saw that our host and hostess took to her immediately, called us 'Three Graces', as is often said when a trio of young females is assembled, and left us alone to speak.

'Well, tell me!', Jane said. —'No, you tell', I said, then listened to her babbling discourse, hunter on the track and trail of every word, as Jane was, too, hands clenched and leaning forward, lips apart.

There had been no explosion, Julie said. Mama had blamed Papa for all, and he had been at a loss to make reply, or so said Julie, though I could not imagine that to be.

'And then, and then, and then?', I asked again, again.

'He said I was to come and see that you were well, both well, and make report as to your comfort and your company—and, well, when you know yourself to be of one mind, to return home, if you wish, or else to let him know what you intend'.

'Julie, you won't tell him everything?'

'Of course, you silly, no—of course I won't. I shall say that you are happy and in company with modesty, and...'

'Even if you have to say your prayers again?', asked Jane, and looked betwixt a frown and smile.

'Ha! What a one to talk *you* are! Emily has more trust in me than that. I have been naughty since and shall be more again—but what has that to do with it?'

'Darlings, have you finished? Is all well? Julie, you will stay with us tonight, I hope. I could not help but overhear what was just said—forgive me—but there will be fun', said Aramintha, peeping head into the bedroom where we sat.

Julie would stay, I said. I had forgiven her her 'prayers', having now said my own with some abandon. Thereat we spent a pleasant day, confessing many things we might not otherwise have done, though I said naught of Jenkins' bout with me which stirred my loins still when I thought of it. A curiosity was upon me to meet his daughters, though I doubted it were possible. All of us are voyeurs in our minds and find delight in seeking sins with lanterns in the dark rooms of others' lives.

There was much giggling, nudging, when we dressed for dinner, but the meal was by all standards brief.

'Do not have a full belly nor an empty one when you make love', said Aramintha. 'Let the wine mingle pleasantly with what you have within and you will be the more prepared to. Now, girls, look at your most sedate, for that is what is required at first. You have no drawers on, none of you, I trust? Well, good'.

Her frank words made me wriggle, as they did the other two. We quaffed liqueurs, patted our hair, and waited till the carriages arrived, wheels crunching on the gravel, and the soft hullos of guests arriving while we sat like waxen maidens, wearing artificial smiles.

The guests were only six. I had expected more: a full concourse, an overcrowded drawing room. Three gentlemen, three ladies. All were roughly of the age of Aramintha, neither young nor old. Names were exchanged, but only Christian ones. One lady, in particular—Elizabeth—attracted me. Her hair was long and dark, her face betwixt the round and oval, with lustrous lips and huge, dark eyes. There being no ceremony whatever, she perched upon the side of my armchair and ran her fingers all around my neck—'finger-whispering', as she called it afterwards.

'Is it not pleasant to be in a house where one can make free?', she asked. Jane was already being kissed, and Julie, too—they also by other ladies while the men waited, watched, and smoked cigars.

'I like it, yes', I answered, conscious that I was like a violin that was being gently tuned.'

'I was your age when I began to do the same', she murmured, and her velvet mouth touched mine, moved sideways slowly, and then drew away, leaning on sideways to me, and my chin upraised. 'You have a lovely mouth. The first thing is to learn to kiss. Were you taught that? Come, slide down on the floor and let us kiss. Show no timidity. A girl here once—your junior...'

'Yes, I heard', said I. My dress rucked as I slid, bumped on the floor, uncovering my knees. With a soft laugh she fell upon me, edged her own gown up and put a knee between my legs, was over me like a slim bird of prey.

'My husband will have you first. You do not mind?'

Before I could reply, she was gobbling up my lips with her warm own, one hand beneath my head, the other stealing up my thighs.

'You do not need to look at him. He likes to see my mouth upon a girl's while he is fucking her. I have the feel of what he likes, you see, and thus we stay in

114

love. Extend your tongue—he likes to see them touch. Open your legs more. Let me get your gown up underneath your bottom, dear'.

I wanted, wanted to say no. Her mouth was sweet, though, and her tongue agile. My bush was bared. I gurgled as she touched my quim, parted the dark, thick curls, the lips. Around, above us, kisses sounded, whispers, moans. Her finger circled suavely round my spot and made me jerk. Under the liquid velvet of her mouth I breathed.

'I have to hold you while he puts it in. It is the way of men—or some. But let us rub first; he adores to see my bottom up', came her soft voice, and then between my legs she slid, pressed back my knees, and squirmed the soft lips of her quim to mine.

I managed to gasp 'HAAR!', but then her mouth was mashed again to mine, tongue twirling, rubbing slowly up and down between my legs, brush of her pubic bush to mine, soft face between my wondering palms, and a cacophony of passion all around. I heard my sister squeal, 'Nah! OH! Not in my b . . . b . . . bottom! OOOH!', but then her cry merged in with others just as lewd. Our stocking tops were rubbing: silk of thighs to silk, our bellies smooth as oil together as she churned, then of a sudden bit my neck and shimmered out her spendings, as I did in turn. Our fingers bit into each other's arms. I knew the scent of her, the perfume musky from between her thighs.

'Make me come more', I whimpered—knew it not to be my voice.

'She is ready, then, Elizabeth. Roll off of her and hold her shoulders down—and do it quickly, woman, dammit, for my prick is stiff', I heard. Then light invaded once again my eyes and I saw the man who stood above, naked of all save for his shirt, his penis rampant—heavy, hairy balls.

'Oh no, oh no, Elizabeth!', I begged. It was too

soon, too sudden and too sharp. A haze of lust was on me, yet I wanted more of her own comforting—wanted a woman's tongue, lips, thighs—wanted the squishy rubbing of our quims.

'Hold her, I said!'

'Yes, darling, yes!'.

She sprang up kneeling at my side and pressed my shoulders firmly with her hands while I, glaze-eyed, stared back at her. Her face was all faces—Julie's, Jane's and Constance's.

'Make me come again', I repeated. The utterance was mindless, but I did not care. I did not wish to see him more, and so meshed my lips beneath her own, feeling him kneel between my calves, feeling him come down upon me with a grunt and nub his prick between my oily lips. I remember the stamen-thrusts of him, full sheathing up at first without a pause, then moving strongly back and forth. And I remember her tongue and the baring of my breasts, which both their fingers managed. I was ridden lustily, my bottom bumped and bumping, and the dusty carpet and the cries and moans around, and then he came, too soon, too soon, the powerful, splashing shoot, his balls tight under to my bulbing derriere, and held there, letting it spurt in.

At the last, at the last—although I did not want—he brushed his wife aside and mouthed his mouth on mine; and although I say I did not want, I knew a strange and uninvited thrill in his lying full weight on me, prick a-pulsing still and tongue within my mouth, I pressed flat down.

'OH-WOH!', I heard Jane cry out in that instant. One gentleman had succeeded another in pistoning her bottom and undoubtedly he must have found a foamy home therein. Julie was busy sucking on a cock while Harry nested in her quim. All three of us were being put 'to homely use' as afterwards was said. I thought the phrase dismissive, but Jane and Julie did not. 'After all, there is a grain of truth in it', said Jane. I put out my tongue at her.

'It means we are owned', I said.

'In part we are—but what's to that if we are being pleasured well?', she countered.

But that was two days afterwards, I being one who sometimes broods on things and then repeats them later.

My conqueror had meanwhile risen, cock-adrip in that heavy way it does. His naked toes stirred sensuously up and down my stockinged legs, he gazing down on me appraisingly.

'Such silky skin, such firmness everywhere', he murmured, making me feel like a filly rather than a girl.

'She must visit us. I love her mouth', his wife said, and continued leaning over me with quite a tender smile, brushed back my hair and kissed the corner of my mouth.

'Let me sit up', I said. I had gained possession of myself once more. My cunny throbbed agreeably. I shifted up and placed my back against the chair-seat. Jane—in a sweet agony—was receiving then her second spoutings, kneeling up upon a chair, her bottom poised to the invading prick. I saw with awe her orifice gripped like a baby's mouth around the rigid stem. Julie lay prone. Her lips were creamy, and her cunny no less so.

'She looks like you', the woman said of Jane, and asked, 'Are you sisters?'

'Yes', I said. I wanted the room to move away from me, and all to vanish.

'Good. Then you will both come and see us; I do hope you will'.

'I want to pee', I whispered and got up. The floor rocked a little underneath my feet.

'Sometimes he likes to watch us pee', the woman said. She made to get up with me, but I brushed her hand away. It is best to be unspeaking sometimes; sometimes it is best. The words that are not said are often the best words.

Jane uttered up a little 'OOOOH!' and was uncorked. Hearing, I heard, but did not look, and passed into the hall and was about to mount the stairs when voices came from a side room.

'Bad show, yes, about Smithers', I heard a deep voice say, and recognised it for that of Jenkins, but of a different tone, and with an accent level with the other man's who then replied to some effect that one should pay one's gambling debts.

'Absolutely, old fellow', Jenkins said. I heard them make to exit and stepped quickly into the morning room where the half open door concealed me as they passed.

Waiting till they had gone, I slipped without and stole upstairs. My need to pee had grown on me. I could not even wait to close the closet door. No sooner had I sat upon the bowl than Aramintha swept in, I gurgling out my wine and punch into the waiting water.

She closed the door, knelt quickly inbetween my open legs, soothed both hands up my thighs to clasp my naked hips and murmured, 'Kiss me!'

Awkward as the posture was, I bent. Mouths met. My belly tingled, straining.

'Open your legs more', she insisted up against my mouth and, as I did, she slipped her slim hand inbetween the porcelain's cold rim and cupped my lovelips to receive their golden rain. Had I not done this before?, she asked. I shook my head between our kissings, squirted yet again and felt it flow upon her fingers, felt a luxury of sin in my still lingering naivete. Drawing me up, she brought my wet thighs to her own uncovered ones, wearing as she was but a chemise and stockings. —'Nice! There are so many things you have to learn', she said, then spun us both around and sat in turn, and insisted that I did the same to her.

O sparkling rills! The strange act quite excited me; I knew not why, the splashing of her pee upon my palm. A relative, she said, had taught her this and made her piss upon his hand when she was young. Then he would raise her bodily up from the toilet seat and make her young legs wind around his waist, lowering her wet cleft slowly down to meet his rampant prick until it sheathed within her.

'Sometimes he made me pee first on his cock, or sometimes on his chest. How wet we were!', she laughed, and rose and wiped us both with a soft sponge.

'Jenkins', I said.

She knew immediately; she knew.

'Have you uncovered him?', she laughed, and I had nothing left to hide.

'Twice over now, but in two different ways. I heard him speaking downstairs with a friend of yours'.

'Oh, as to that . . . Well, yes—we have dissembled, I confess. He loves to play the role of servitor, and much good does it do him, as you know. It is a fair way to thread the ladies who come here to seek adventure, on the quiet'.

'His daughters, though; he is very roguish, is he not?', I asked.

'Along *that* road you travelled with him then? I must confess, it is his favourite sport. But daughters, no; he has none, in real truth. 'Tis all a fantasy that he enjoys. He has his own estate not far from here. Men have their foibles, dear. You must play up to them in order that you profit most. I have known dear Charles (yes, that is his real name), oh, on and off for years and years. Shall you tell him that you know? I do not mind, and nor will he, but if you are clever, Emily, you will play his little game just a bit more—though always have a hook in what you do'.

'A hook?', I echoed.

'He thinks himself to be the fisherman, my pet. His

only trick, though, is to play the role of a rough servitor and work on such susceptibilities as he can find. He has not missed his role as an actor, as some might say, for he plays it on the stage of life itself. He has two sons. I vow that had he had a daughter, he would never dared have touch her. Harry does not agree with me but I think that. Hence if you fulfill his dream, he must reward you. That is your hook: the fisherman is caught!'

'I shall not come down again', I said, whereat she tilted her head quite prettily and gave me a sympathetic smile.

'I am not wanting a needlessly long night, either, Emily. I will soon see them off, in any case. Elizabeth asks after you. May I say that you will visit her?'

'I may; I do not know; I may'. I edged towards the closet door; she followed.

'I will ask Jenkins to move your empty baggage', Aramintha said. I could feel the smile her lips did not produce. Her back towards me, she went quickly down.

CHAPTER 14

I have heard the cries of the forlorn who often say, 'I am at the crossroads of my life', and look to one to give directions. Being of occasionally morbid mind, I envisage immediately four muddy, empty roads, some flanked by trees and others by broad fields, and all an emptiness, a lonely sea of mud and waiting wet the farmers have deserted. There are no signposts. No one else invades that misty scene of silent grass, and fog amid the boughs of trees deserted by the birds. A cloaked and timourous one arrives, lamp held with little hope and—having cast around and finding neither light nor dark but only that unease that lies between the two—takes hopelessly upon one of the tracks towards an horizon that ever further moves away, away, oh on and on, the long, long lea away.

Morbidity, however, brings me to desire. Moods come upon me when I wish to be slothful, desire to be unclothed almost against my will, and bundled, badgered, coaxed into being mounted, then to feel the stinging, surging, soothing of the prick inside my cunny, lying plaintive underneath the heaving male.

I think of myself thus as 'being worked'. I do not mind. I may by turns, by other wendings of my mind, be maid or mistress, wife or daughter, whore or nun. So many words and actions can excite in changing roles.

Whether I would see Elizabeth again or whether I would cast myself in the path of Jenkins, I did not know, and slept on it. Upon the morrow, however, the false manservant had left, or had appeared to do so by his

absence. That small thing decided me. I had used the
house for a moment, had been used in it as well. Even
so, it had a comfort and an *ambiance* I liked, and hence
I said to Aramintha that I would visit Elizabeth that
afternoon. Her house being but four miles from theirs,
I would return in several hours, I said.

'If you then wish to, Emily, yes, but take your nightgown just in case', she smiled.

'Oh pouf! Your mind runs in one channel, Aramintha!', I replied, but even so I sneaked a toothbrush
in my reticule.

Was it a journey that I really wished to make? I was
not sure, but even so it got me out into the world again.
Fears, wonderings, desires, doubts, hesitations, all mingle in the mind, and to no purpose usually, for what
will occur will occur once the right foot has moved a
single step before the left.

Elizabeth greeted me with great pleasure in a drawing room far too ornate for my taste. Her husband was
away, she said, though uttered it with some relief. All
the time speaking, all the time speaking, she stood close
to me and touched my face, my breasts, my thighs.

'I was itching for you to come again, and you have
chosen the right day: a perfect day, in fact. I thought
of you, upstairs just now, and wished you here'.

'Upstairs?'

I have occasionally an empty, foolish habit in repeating words.

'Indeed, and I will show you. Fortunately he is very
quiet. One has to depend so much upon discretion,
does one not? I love your grey dress—how it moulds
your breasts and shows your bottom to perfection, Emily. Come—the young man in question will delight
you; I am sure of that'.

'The young...?'

I wished to say it only in my mind. The words
spilled out.

'He is fifteen, my pet'. She had already begun to lead me out again, and then went on in hushed and solemn tones, 'He has the most beautiful Mama you could ever see, but the silly woman has no fancies such as we evolve and toy with and make true. The dear boy wants to but she will not let me, and complained to me of his behaviour—peeping in her boudoir, and all such. He has had his hands a little up her clothes and kissed her, but she will not donate her tongue nor let his fingers touch her drawers. How wasteful, Emily! Do you not think it is?'

The question took me by surprise.

'I do not know', I said, and halfway up the broad stairway she paused and tucked her arm about my waist.

'That which is known need not have been experienced. In the mind, all things are known, and therein frequently are done. When one lets go, lets go, ah then, the splendour and the daring rise. Do not tell me you have not tasted the forbidden fruit!'

We had stayed ourselves, my back against the bannisters. A waiting quiet, like a deep breath with-held, waited above: a panther without form, as I thought of it.

'No, I have . . . Yes, I have', I murmured truthfully enough. Poor James—I had so flirted with him, teased. Mary had sucked his cock and I had loved to see it done. Pale face, his sweet face, and his lips to mine. No one had held my bottom boldly before Papa had done.

'You see! I knew it! We are really of one mind—can even speak of it, and no harm done. May I tell you that I love you, and that I love to see you being done, as *much* as I would have you to myself? Lick my tongue now, for a moment, Emily, and be obedient, but at other times . . .'

'Yes, what?', I asked and laughed and licked her long, pink tongue luxuriously.

'At other times be bold, you sillikins. Speak what you want to speak. Speak now of the first thing that comes to you'.

I was conscious of the waiting up above, and yet more of the resilience of her breasts to mine. Such consciousness brought words into my head.

'I like to see my sister with a cock in her', I said, and hated myself for the crudeness of my words, yet Elizabeth but smiled.

'You will see my husband on her soon enough. I will smack her first, then bring her bottom to his prick. What fun! But come now, I am already moist at all these naughty thoughts. I swear you are!'

Lips loosed themselves. My hand was taken. I was sped beyond on to the landing and then towards a boudoir where the door was just ajar. Pushing it open boldly, Elizabeth drew me in and closed the door.

The youth lay naked on the bed: a girlish boy with narrow hips, eyelashes not unlike a girl's, and tousled hair as if he had fretted there for long. Beside him lay a pair of long white drawers his fingers clasped.

'They are his Mama's, the poor sweet. See how still he lies and waits. His teeth are perfect and his breath is sweet. I have seen to that with milk and bonbons, haven't I?', she asked him, and he blinked, first nervously at her and then at me, then nodded. As for myself, I felt almost a motherliness towards him, for he looked so unguarded to the world, and yet I felt too a sense of excitement at his passive waiting, arms down at his sides and cock erect.

'His balls are small—almost like plover's eggs—and yet he comes with fair abundance for his age. Bend over—feel them—Emily. No—wait! Strip to your stockings and I will do the same. He will not move at all until we touch him, and then becomes a little fury. One can tame him quickly, though, by bringing him to spend, and then he likes to cuddle with his cock all limp and wet between one's thighs. Oh dear, what things young boys *will* get up to these days!'

Her hands were at her clothing as she spoke, though first she had unbuttoned me, loosed all the buttons down my back, then—swooping up her own pink gown—showed wondrous pearly thighs above her stocking tops.

'Quickly!', she laughed and, casting off her dress, revealed herself to have been naked underneath. And what a wondrous form she had! Her hips had that 'violin curve' that makes a woman so desirable. Her belly curved but slightly. Underneath was a dark thatch luxuriant with curls. Her breasts were perfect melons—ruby nipples set upon the cream of her fine skin, the mounds aggressive, jiggling as she moved and waited for my own uncovering which took not but a moment more.

We faced each other—faced each other in a moment of desire, and had no need to speak of it. I felt her belly fitting close to mine before it even did. Three steps and we were touching nipples, manoeuvering our thighs to let our bushes touch.

'Boldness becomes you, Emily, to stand so. Have you done so always? You must tell me more about yourself. Mouth open now—receive my tongue. Move closer backwards to the bed and let him sniff your bottom while we kiss. I promise you he'll do no more than that, until I say. Darling, my love, what lovely bottom cheeks you have. I trust you have received intruders there?'

'Yes', I said faintly. Cloudily her mouth came on my own. We swayed, moved backwards, dragging feet. I heard the youth shift and tensed myself. His body rolled behind me on the bed. I felt the breathing of his breath close to my offered hemispheres.

'A little sniffing does him good, for he will know the scent of you henceforth', Elizabeth murmured.

I confess to a squeak then, for as she spoke and

squashed my mouth to hers, so the youth's nose intruded, searching like a tiny dog to poke between my nether cheeks and rummage, hotly breathing, at my hole.

'Is he there?', Elizabeth asked softly to my lips.

'Mmmmm....', I hummed against her own. His nose was moving as a gentle finger moves, around the puckered rim and up and down. I waited for his tongue, but felt no touch of it.

'He may not lick you less you wish him to'.

Her voice was husky, urgent, tickling on my lips. I sensed her need that I should follow on the path her words had laid and bulbed my bottom more and felt as wickedly obscene as I had done with Jenkins on the bed.

'Want him to lick me there', I murmured, drawing in my breath and thus her own which flowed upon my tongue.

'Excellent! The posture must be quite exact, my pet. It is one of both obedience and offering we teach to younger girls sometimes. May I show you, Emily? Oh, do say yes!'

I assented softly. There was safety here. I felt love lambent in her lips and knew it to be so. Upon my whispering yes, she moved to one side of me and placed her fingertips beneath my chin, exhorting me to bend my body forward and thus thrust out my bottom all the more. But she had asked, not forced me to the trick.

I did so—felt a mischief in the stance, my legs apart, eyes facing forward at the wall, her hand quite firm but comforting that held my head up. Tenderly, with her free hand, she tickled up my nipples one by one and then softly exhorted the boy to lick whatever he could find.

I quivered as I felt his tongue. It roamed the bulbing surfaces at first, sauntered into the cleft, retreated, licked around again, and then returned to toil and tingle round

my orifice. It swirled, it dipped. He had been taught—
as I later realised—the *feuille de rose* wherein the tongue
is pointed, curled each side upon itself, and so brought
to intrude within. When a young girl is teased thus—
one who had not then taken cock, but is to be persuaded
to—a stout bar is held across her thighs to prevent her
jerking forward. Three women attend her: one holds
up her chin (standing in front of her) while the others
hold the bar or—equally—may hold her arms stretched
out on either side. The male attends her bottom then
with tongue, or it may be another girl who will as
equally enjoy her little moans and cries.

'He has his tongue in, hasn't he?', Elizabeth asked.

'Mmmm... MMMMMM!', was all that I could
say. The warm tickling, the invasion, was delicious,
sending further, gentle tongues of flame throughout my
belly. I sniffled, snuffled, rolled my eyes. Elizabeth
laughed agreeably. Taking her hand from under my
stiff-nippled breasts, she evidently grasped the boy's head
at the back and forced his face more into me, making
me breathe more deeply and causing him to splutter
so that I felt the spatterings of his saliva everywhere.

'Are you ready to receive him, Emily? Move back—
lie down upon your hip!', she uttered to him sharply.

As he did, she gently urged me on my back upon
the bed, wet bottom facing into him, then slumped
beside me in her turn, sharp nipples to my own and
face to face.

'Just kiss. He loves to hear the sound', she said.
Wet-lapping were our tongues together while the youth's
prick ticked its urgency against my bottom cheeks. He
did not stir, though, did not stir. 'Clasp me tightly,
Emily, for I am going to hold you by the waist', she
murmured and, with that, did so and cupped my springy
bottom cheeks and held them wide apart to him.

'GOOO!', I choked next, for then his knob slipped
in, push-probing through the rimhole of my rose and

seeking tightly upwards in its path. The veins on his slim penis throbbed. I gripped him of a mischief, with four inches in, and then let him proceed as inch by inch he urged his syringe up between my cheeks.

'Nice? Is it nice? Say it is nice?', came Elizabeth's cooing voice against my lips.

'Nnnnng!', I gritted for, with that, he pistoned it full in. I felt her hand beneath my cunny tickling both his balls. His tummy slapped against my bottom hard.

'L...let me kiss you!', came a whine, he panting warm breath on my shoulder then. I thought him to mean me, and in the swimming pleasure turned my face, but Elizabeth's brushed past my cheek to push her lips to his and I between them tightly sandwiched. —'Mer-mer-mer-mer!', he moaned. I heard the sibilance of meeting tongues and worked my bottom to his gliding thrusts, my tube so close-clenched around his prick.

'Bugger her, darling—do it to her nicely, though. You little devil, if I let you. . . . OOOH!'

Desire had overcome her and she sprinkled on my amourous hand, her bush crushed down upon my palm. I felt her ecstasy and then was coming on myself, dizzy with white light—the most exquisite of sensations as that youthful syringe pulsed and pumped the more, the three of us a-panting and the sounds of tongues and lips.

'Mama!, I'm coming!', the youth moaned. His cork swelled for a moment up between my springy cheeks and half drew out. Then, pistoning full in again, he loosed his fine and bubbly jets, a-gasping as he was into her mouth, my breasts full bulged to hers, our nipples thorns.

'HAAAR! Do it to her, darling—yes—right up!'

My feet kissed hers, knees bumped, and I received his final jets within my sucking orifice, he moaning much as if he were in pain, but really in that hot, volcanic pleasure that comes when all the juices flow and flesh is stung with sweetness of release. A-bubble-bubble came his weaker spurts, then he was done. The fleshy slug ticked in me still and then withdrew with a faint 'Plop!'

'Oh god, that was delicious!', came my sigh. I felt the boy roll from me, weakly stir.

'There! Was it not? The advantages of youth, my pet. He will get his corker up in half an hour, or less, if he's encouraged', said Elizabeth.

We rolled upon our bottoms—all lay hips to hips. I moved my right hand idly and touched the boy's moist prick and felt his balls. Then of a sudden I recalled his cry and rolled upon Elizabeth and held her down, her belly quivering underneath my own.

'He is your son!', I said.

'Oh no, he's not! He loves to call me Mama since I nourish his desires so well'.

'He looks like you a little—yes, he does!' I swung my head sideways and kissed the boy. His lips were like a girl's and trembled underneath my own.

'Oh, really, Emily! Imagine if he were. You think I would permit such naughtiness?'

'I do indeed, you witch!', I laughed. My nose rubbed to her own again, my eyes explored her deep blue ones and so much mischief glimmering in their depths.— 'Oh tell me—honestly'. I knew I could not ask the youth who had half turned in shyness.—'You said he had a *beautiful* Mama', I wheedled, urging my quim-hairs deep into her own.

'I did? Would I make such?', she teased, and I not knowing whether to believe or not.

'He does it to you, though?'

'Sometimes, of course, I let him, yes. I make him do it to me standing up, my back against the wall, knees bent. How lewd it feels! I swear I will coax her into letting him, someday'.

'Suck his penis now, Elizabeth. I want to see'.

'Oh!' Even as she gasped, however, so she rolled from under me, curled up—I kneeling, looking down at them. The boy stirred at her touch, stared up at me, eyes open wide, and uttered a pathetic little whine as her velvet lips enclosed his sticky knob.

CHAPTER 15

I did not stay, although she coaxed me to. Her husband would return. I did not wish to meet him then, nor ever perhaps again. The youth had fucked her while I watched—a wriggling fish upon her belly as he worked and cried his little cries of joy, prick moving back and forth within her quim, clawing at her plump bottom as he did.

Not long after we had dressed, repaired ourselves, a carriage came. A lady sat within. I saw her face but mistily. The boy ran out and clambered in, she giving an imperious wave and then was gone.

'She does not mind? How curious', said I.

'The minds of those we do not know are even more curious than ours, my dear. She regards me as his wet-nurse, I believe', she laughed, then asked me much about myself, though cautiously and with discretion that I valued. Thus I took to her the more. Several adventures of her own she told me. All were lewd, and yet not spoken with crude tongue. I told her how Papa had found me with my drawers down, and she laughed.

'He is to be complimented much upon his taste. You are less bold than Myrtle or the other one', she said, for I had given Jane's name so.

'He was almost bold with me. Not quite. I wondered at it, at the time'. I ventured, and she read the question in my eyes.

'*Almost* is tenderness. Remember that. And should you ever come to it again. . . .

'I won't', I said too quickly, and she shook her head.

'Betwixt tenderness and boldness is a pleasant path,

Emily. Men grapple with one sometimes, force one over. In particular in youth they do, and gain the measure of your bottom or your slit, sometimes by forcing, sometimes wheedling in a foolish way—or sometimes after birching one. Many a girl has flowered upon an urgent cock that way, and is no worse for it. Once it is done, it's done. There come the heaving sighs, the pants—the sperm releases and the honeypot receives. Remember how I told you... up against the wall? It teased both him and me, my drawers—yes, drawers!— down to my knees, my thighs not quite apart as he had wished, my dress held up just like a little girl who's made to show for the first time. Awkward it was, yet thrilling—I can tell you that. His nose was thrust between my breasts. I held him tightly as he came. Afterwards I scolded him, for that is what he really likes, and looks most mournful till you cuddle him again'.

I listened fascinated to her words. They led me also into corridors of thought beyond my own—into the heads of others, so to speak. One thinks of one's own pleasures mainly, not of others. That's the pity of world, though pleasures must be mutual, of course. I said such to her, and she gave as much thought to my words as I had to hers.

'There are many ways to reach the peaks of pleasure, Emily. I thought it very naughty when my uncle made me raise my skirts, wanted to close my legs and hide myself. In the first moment that he put his cock to me, I felt a terror and would have resisted had he not been implacable and held my hips so tightly while he urged it up. Pleasure does not come at the first touch always. I mean, at the first touch to mind *or* body—don't you see?'

'Jane... I mean, Myrtle... she was whipped', I said. I said it to provoke; I knew I did.

'Jane is her real name? Good. I'm glad you told me that. I know both your names now. Yes, mine *is* Elizabeth! If Jane were whipped then I have no doubt she needed it, within herself I mean. Girls sometimes must be made to do that which they never otherwise would do. Boys, too, occasionally!', she laughed, and told me how her brother had been spanked when they were young and how his prick had got quite stiff until their governness had teased him off and made him spurt across her stocking tops.

'Well—you have all my secrets now', I said, and rose to go.

'I have gathered all the roses from your mind... and the buds, too?', she teased. 'Come to me whenever you have a problem, Emily. I promise you that I will do the same'.

'Oh, but I do not know enough to counsel you!'

'You know more than you think, my pet. Dwell on the moment that my husband mounted you. You did not quaver, howl or kick. Quite properly you took his prick. Dwell on the moment when you refused your tastings, and quite properly. 'Twas clever of you, that, and made you even more desirable in such eyes as would have uncovered your sweet thighs and bottom. Dwell on the moment when your Papa found you with your drawers down and should have swept his hand up underneath your skirt'.

'Oh! *Elizabeth*!', I gasped.

'Oho! You had not thought of it before?', she teased, and with a fond kiss I departed. Dear Elizabeth—she could say almost anything to me, and never raised my hackles ever once.

Scarce had my carriage gone a mile than the horses began to slow and I looked out, gliding my window down to see why we were stopping. There, ahead, sat Jenkins on a horse, his hand held up. Wheeling his steed, he came alongside and looked down on my enquiring face.

'A fair day, Miss'.

'You followed me', I said and was about to tell my driver to go on when Jenkins leaned down from his horse and held the windowsill.

'Forgive me—for you know the truth of my identity, I know. I wished but to apologise'.

'Oh? Why to me? Am I the fairest of them all?', I sneered.

'You have the softest voice, the loveliest of limbs. Fairest of form and face you are indeed—and I your servitor, your true one now. Pray, will you not take tea with me, or something a trifle stronger, wine perhaps? My house...'

'I do not wish....' I halted back my words, conserved my smile. 'I am expected back', I said, and thought that for a silly thing to say. It meant that someone other was directing me. I did not wish to be seen to be in his eyes, nor any other man's. —'A half an hour. That is all that I will allow you', I then said, and half despite myself. My bottom tingled just a little still from the boy's prick, or else my imagination made me think it so.

'Thank you. A thousand thanks! Then I will lead the coachman. It is but a short ride on from here. A half an hour in heaven will be worth a year on earth', he said, but looked more timourous than pleased, the actor in him or the hidden man emerging. Both, perhaps.

I was thankful that we did not have to speak again during the interval that passed, the hedges flashing green beneath my eyes, my consciousness of him upon the saddle, broad. And that enormous... No... I should not dwell on that, I thought—but not to dwell on something is, as Papa has since said to me, like having a monkey on one's shoulder that one wishes to ignore, but cannot for it moves this way and that and makes its presence ever felt.

Charles. I would call him Charles, in a cold tone.

Would sit, cup held, and little finger curled, would act Miss Prim and put him off his sport. . . .

Such were my ponderings, and yet how hard it is to put on a face, a voice, one does not have. The mind moves on to neutral ground and waits, as mine did on arrival. A fair mansion was it, lying back in its own acres. Over a hundred, as he told me proudly over tea. I had insisted on the tea. Wine would have meant conviviality. The drawing room was plain—had little of a woman's touch. Among the likenessess upon the mantelpiece I saw one of two girls and asked, as coyly as I might, were these his daughters?

'Yes', he said, I biting back a smile, for Aramintha had not told him all.

'They are pretty—very pretty'. I got up to look at them, and heard him move as I expected, coming up behind me till my bottom nestled to his loins.

'No more than you—the fairest of the three', said he. I squeezed my eyes up tight, then opened them, but did not turn my head.

'Mama is still away?', I asked, and heard the catching of his breath.

The room was still, the room was still.

'Yes', he said thickly, palmed my hips and felt their curves.

'For long?', I asked—a catch in my own voice.

He could not breathe—I swear he could not breathe. I felt the tautness of his chest, the stirrings of his penis through his trouser cloth.

'For long enough to bed you as I wish, my dear, my dearest little pet', he husked and with that groaned and cupped my bulbing tits, feeling the flesh warm through my thin grey gown.

I drooped my head and stood as one forlorn.

'I want to see Mama. Oh, Papa, you must not', I whined. My nipples budded to his fingers then, already stiffened to his fingers.

'I beg you to stand still a moment thus, letting me hold your breasts, my sweet—I beg you to. Ah—press your darling bottom in. Can you not feel—can you not feel my. . . .'

'No! Oh no! Oh no, it's rude, Papa. If Mama came. . .' I burst from him, spun past his shoulder and sat down again in a deep chair and covered up my face.

'She will not—that I swear!'

He fell upon his knees and clasped my own. I clipped my thighs together and then peeped between face-cupping fingers. Timidly he moved my dress up almost to my knees, then stopped.

'She may', I mumbled. Suddenly I sensed the subtle invitations that he needed—read the words that haunted his dark eyes. —'She would find you kissing me', I said, 'and putting your hand up where you did before, trying to pull my drawers down—yes—you know you did. I was all a-tremble, knew not what to do'.

'Before she came, or after?'

'Both'.

I bit my lip and lowered both my hands, gazing as if in frozen embarrassment as he eased his hands up far beneath my skirt and laid them gently on my silky thighs.

'Don't, Papa, no', I said between clenched teeth, yet did not make to thrust his hands away.

'Just open them, my love, and let me see your furry treasure.'

'No, no, Papa! You dare! What wicked things you say! Mama! Oh, don't!', I squealed.

To my astonishment he then fell back, half fallen on his hip, restored himself, but stayed upon his knees, his prick a massive bulge beneath his cloth. A sob escaped him and he covered up his face. His sobs were real; I sensed them to be so and sat bemused. His shoulders shook. Real tears ran down his face.

'Oh, Papa, don't', I murmured and leaned forward

then and touched his head—felt timourous and quite dismayed. His hands fell slowly from his face. A teardrop glistened just beside his mouth.

'I cannot help myself', he moaned, and looked most piteous, I thought.

I stared for a long moment in his eyes, gathered myself and plucked at my half-raised skirt as if I knew not whether to raise it or to push it down.

'Papa, you may kiss me if you really want', I said, and said it in the voice of some sweet simpleton whose garters he could almost see from down below. Indeed, I saw his eyes go there and moved my legs a little, parting them.

'And touch you? May I touch you inbetween?'

'Oh, Papa, I don't know, I . . . AAAH!'

He was half risen, on me in a flash. One hand swooped up between my open legs and cupped my nest, his mouth aflame on mine. I spluttered, as he wished, and beat his shoulders, but he held me down, elbowed my knees apart the more and, with deep-seeking tongue within my mouth, he found my spot and twiddled it. I snorted, snuffled, whimpered to his mouth. His digit entered inbetween my lovelips, found them moist.

'Come on the floor, my love'.

'No, no—oh, NO!'

One wailing cry and I had tumbled down, he throwing up my skirts above my hips, baring my bottom to the waiting floor while, heavy in girth, he got between my thighs and worked with desperation at his trouser buttons.

I shrieked, I moaned—I turned my face this way and that, his knuckles pressed against my milky skin, fumbling and feeling underneath himself until his enormous penis burgeoned out and brought its crest to quiver at my nest.

'NA-HAAAR!', I squealed. I kicked my legs, but raised them as I did so, which enabled him to sleek his knob between my pouting lips and drive the shaft within with lone long thrust that pinned me like a stricken butterfly.

'HAR! Oh my god, my sweet, my darling daughter, I am in you now. What a soft, furry, oily nest you have!'

'T . . . t . . . take it out, Papa! Oh-WOH!'

Feebly I beat at him and would not take his mouth, twisting my own up with an anguished look, holding a wild look in my eyes that must have seemed to him so real.

'I shall hold you down, my love, until you do', he groaned. His great thick penis did not move. It throbbed superbly in my silken grip.

'Won't, won't!', I sobbed.

'Give me your mouth, my darling, do—a little moment only—then I'll take it out'.

One finger in my mouth—oh artful touch!—and face averted underneath his own, I uttered still my little sobs, then let my expression take on a broody look, his own a cloud of anxious lust. With tenderness he slowly drew my finger from my mouth. I did not move then, waited for his own to touch the corner of my lips, and felt the most exquisite thrill.

'Oh, Papa!'

'Just one little kiss, my sweet'.

'You p . . . p . . . promise me, Papa?' Lips buzzed against each other's as we spoke.

'Open your mouth more. Bring it under mine and let our tongues touch, darling'.

'N . . . n . . . n . . . no, I mustn't. . . . Naughty. . . . Please, Papa . . . HAAAR-OOOH!'

A savagery possessed him then. His mouth mashed to my own, his forearms thrust beneath my thighs, hands strong and urgent underneath my bottom cheeks—the two halves of my apple on his palms. His cock sucked out, thrust in again, ploughing my furrow with a will as if indeed to ram his message home, I flooding sobs and moans into his mouth.

'You beauty—AH! You're coming over Papa's prick', he mouthed, feeling my tingling spurts glide down his prick.

'Yes, no! Oh, I can't help myself! You mustn't, mustn't, mustn't. . . . Oooh yes, OOOH!'

'My little love, my pet, my dove, your cunt is taking Papa's cock at last. Do you not like it? Say you do!'

'Yes, Papa, yes—oh, do it more!' Impassioned were my arms about his neck. My legs coiled up as they had done before, crossed round his waist, and clinging like a child. His moans beseeched my tongue to be more lewd. —'Cock in my cunt, Papa, oh yes!' But I was drifting, drifting out away from all such childish non-sense as his piston worked, oiled by the salutations he received. Mouth open wide, I let him suck upon my tongue and surged my hips as hungrily as his, slap-smack of testicles beneath my globe.

'Ask me to fuck you, darling—quickly—say!'

Oh, by what rote man brings himself to final plea-sure thus! The words are but as cymbals to the violin that plays more sweetly inbetween one's thighs. Each clash of brass brings the crescendo near. And yet the bubblings of saliva twixt our mouths, the shunting of his prick in my tight sheath, the animality of hot desire, brought me to answer him in kind.

'Fuck, fuck, Papa. . . . Oh, do it to me, yes! I want to feel you come, I want to feel!'

The trigger was thus pressed. I wondered if he knew in his mad-whirling thoughts who was beneath him, yet in turn I cared not in that moment who was on me, for the bliss was paramount. In huge great jerks he came, white floods of sperm that jetted up and splashed against my walls, I moaning endlessly to him to do it more and more and more and more . . . until we sank exhausted, quivering, and I beneath him crushed, my legs down straight and splayed out wide on either side of his.

There were no kisses then. He hid his face into my shoulder. I resisted stroking him but merely lay quiescent underneath as though regret were seeping into me. Once more, my face averted, I lay quiet.

'Angel, my angel', came his whisper, but I did not stir.

'Papa, get off me, do—oh please! Ugh! What a horrid mess it makes', I murmured as if awakening from a dream. I made to close my legs, but when they touched his trousers opened them again as if disdain had seized me, or regret.

'I have creamed your cunny, pet, at last. You have more curls there than I thought you have. Your bottom is a dream of bliss, so firm, resilient and bold. How long have I watched it wriggle underneath your gowns'.

His voice was broken, weaker than it was before. The flag was limp but still the battle moved.

'You m...m...mustn't talk to me like that. I'll tell Mama, I will. You're hurting me! I cannot breathe! Oh, please, Papa!'

His cock slipped out from my engaging lovemouth, dripped its pearls upon my thigh. Crouched over me, he turned by force my chin to meet his gaze. My own was cold and distant, though. He read there all he wished to see, I knew. The game had to be renewed, and ever on.

'You will not tell her, dear. I beg you not'. He lumbered up, his thick prick dangling down as though to display it hopefully to me. I covered up myself then in a flash and scrambled to my feet in turn. For a long moment I gave him my most woeful look.

'Promise you won't again', I said. His face looked haggard, like a battle field when all the guns have ceased to fire and dusk falls on the bodies where they lie.

'I promise, yes; I'll try', he mumbled, woebegone.

A silence fell. We gazed each other out, and then eyes fell. The carpet was a dark pool of eternity. His purplish knob, still big, was pendant, sticky with our spendings—the rude witness of the deed. I felt my cunny pulse with longing still. I dragged my feet and stopped. Shoulder to shoulder almost, and the moment held.

'What will you do now?', he placated, voice a-tremble as he spoke.

'I have to go out, Papa—to see my friends. You know I do'.

'Yes, yes, of course'. The hour was limp, as was his prick. He tucked it in again beneath his cloth. Guilt hung on him like a rent flag. One look from me would turn it to desire again. And, knowing that, I knew not how to look or where to turn. The play was over and the act was done.

'What time shall you be back?'

'I do not know'. I did not look at him; I toed the floor, showed my uncertainty as best I could. 'Long before bedtime though, Papa', I ventured, turned my head away and tried to blush.

His hand touched mine. I let my wrist go limp, and did not turn my fingertips to his, but even so he sought them, found them, touched.

'Does not your cunny tingle still?', he asked. His words burst out, without control.

'Pa-PA! I . . . OH!'

He spun me, held me crushed to him, groped down beneath my bottom cheeks and raised me struggling on tiptoe.

'Tonight! You hear me? Or I'll bring the strap to you, my girl'. He raised my chin and gripped it painfully, and forced me to look up into his eyes. My own showed anguish mingled with desire.

'You wouldn't, Papa! No—oh, please! Oh, not that horrid strap again! It burns me and you know it does'.

141

'And to what purpose—eh? Now, answer me!'

'To, to, to make me let you'.

'Well?'

'Oh, please, Papa—I have to go. Don't crush me so'.

'The strap or cock, then—which is it to be? I will have no further nonsense from you now'.

'Yes—yes—all right!'

'Come—say it clear; I wish to hear you say'.

'You're h...h...hurting me, Papa. Yes, yes, all right!' His grip had slackened and I pressed away, stepped back from him and gathered up my hat and reticule.

'What?', he demanded.

I put my bonnet on all in a rush, my fingers trembling visibly. The bizarre occurrence had begun to take on a near reality.

'Wh...what you said'. I giggled it and choked at the same time, rushed to the door and sped along the hall.

'My love!', he called, but I was gone, was gone, my driver starting up as I appeared, and brushing cobwebs from his eyes. He raised his whip in readiness. I smiled at him and tumbled in.

He little knew the gesture he had made.

CHAPTER 16

I said nothing to the others of my new encounter with that strange and yet magnetic man. Had I thought less of him, I would. I felt a pity for his state, the utter loneliness that must enfold him in between the stagings of the same play on and on, his grapplings for the words he wished to hear from the mouths of whimpering girls whose legs he spread. Perhaps it was a case of age and youth, I thought, but then remembered James' warm, eager eyes, his hands that groped me up beneath my skirt, and knew it not to be so.

'Shall we not go home?', I asked of Jane the next morning when Julie said she had to leave. Her uncle was to come for her: an invasion by a visitor from a far world.

'I suppose so', Jane said. She had a feeling in her, as she said, that she wished to go somewhere, do something, but she knew not what it was nor where: a sensation not unfamiliar to me, too, and one that stirs me often still, like a branch that shakes itself in a wild wind, pretending it would leave the mother trunk.

'We shall have cock wherever we go—that is for certain', Julie said. Her tone was placid, and no smiling wrinkles round her eyes. Sometimes she had solemnity and was not always fey and bright. But her moods, like those of mine and Jane's, were ever at a change. I was to see a new side to her now, but knew it not until we disengaged ourselves from Harry and Aramintha and went off.

'It may rain today', said Julie's Uncle Herbert in the carriage, she beside him and we facing them.

He was a small man who forever preened himself, wore silk cravats and purple spats, and had but a nibbler of a moustache upon his upper lip.

'It may or it may not. We shall know it if the cows lie down. Be quiet. I have not said that you might speak. My friends, dear Uncle, are not as you think, and will not have your sauciness'.

If one can hear another gape, then I heard Jane do so. My own face flushed. I knew not where to look—her words so brusque. She whom Papa had carried limp and willing from our bed to say her prayers so many weeks before. I expected her uncle to bluster or to shout. Instead he looked more meek and bowed his head. The motions of the carriage jolted him more than it did myself.

'What were we talking of?', asked Julie to me then, as though he were not there.

I covered up confusion by replying something quite mundane. Her uncle raised his face and was expressionless. A tubular protrusion showed between his thighs. I must have stared at it, for Julie laughed and said, 'He likes to have his quietness when with ladies. Do you not?', she asked him, and he nodded, dumb. Thereat she placed her hand upon his thigh and put her thumb upon his covered tool whose knob outlined itself beneath the cloth. —'In a moment we shall stop to have a drink', she said, and called out something to the driver who then hollered back.

Julie sat quietly then—sat like a queen. Her thumb brushed back and forth. Each time it did, her uncle quivered and compressed his lips. His eyes were pebbles—were expressionless. I stared at passing fields on one side—Jane the other. A desire came over me to smack Julie; I knew not why. The impudent power that she exploited puzzled me and set me all awry. I knew not whence it came and sensed that Jane was equally bewildered—tense with an unknowing.

144

We need not stop so soon, I wished to say, but did not speak for fear of an embarrassing reply. I felt as if all were a knot that I could not untie. Five minutes passed along the dusty road, and then the coach wheeled in and stopped outside an inn. Its keeper stood, arms folded, gazed upon our vehicle and then went in as though to lay a carpet down.

Julie got out the first—then I and Jane. Her uncle stayed within, stayed sat. His penis was more prominent from her sly thumbings.

'He will wait', said Julie, and no sooner had we reached the door than she began to giggle, rushed within the rather dark interior and took up seat at a rough table.

'What?', Julie asked. It sounded like a general question to the world at large.

'Oh, he has been like that for years. You must not think it over-bold or strange of me. My aunt has trained him', Julie quaintly said, and ordered white wine for the three of us.

I wanted to tell that he was a man. The male was paramount. That had for long been dinned into our minds. Papa had pushed his trousers down. Julie had knelt with maidenly obedience and...

'Tell us!', said Jane across my thoughts.

'Oh, what's to tell? He does as he is told. Only be females though. I do not understand it much myself. He has a perky strut with other men, quaffs whiskey well and shoots and smokes cigars, and yet...'

'Yet, *what*?', I asked, my nose all wrinkled up.

'Oho, you have seen for yourself. My aunt says he is childlike in the female grip. Many a time she smothers him between her thighs while talking with another lady in their house. He kneels obedient, his face between. When she releases him at last, oh you should see his cheeks, how red they are!'

'Oh!', I ejaculated. So did Jane. The mastery of

Jenkins on me, yet he too had cried. Were males so pliable beneath? I could not bring myself to think they were as frail as we. The world and all its people jumbled in my head. Elizabeth's husband saying 'Hold her down!' —and Aramintha's uncle...Ah...Ah yes. She said that she had peed down on his chest. I had not even pictured it when she said that, but now I did, and felt a strange, warm flush.

'He would wait an hour if I told him so—but come, this is just a lesson to him', Julie said and emptied quick her glass, we leaving ours half drunk and going out into the sun again.

'Have you ever peed on him?', I asked. The words escaped me, sudden as they were. I would not have her think me wholly ignorant.

'Aha! You know!', she laughed, 'Yes, sometimes, yes. How messy, though, it is. He has to lie down in the bath without his trousers on, his shirt tucked up. He has a fair prick on him, not too small. You soon will see'.

'I never thought', said Jane, and then she stopped. We had seen our uncle only several times, and that when we were younger. He had been no more than just an adult shape, a voice, within the house. So many came and went—we took no note, and in any case were ushered early into bed for reasons I had long since understood.

Uncle Herbert sat erect in every sense, cock tenting up his trouser front. A holy silence was maintained as we drove on. I felt it must not break, and so did Jane, for she said nothing, too. I did not mind; I had so much to dwell upon. In fifteen minutes we arrived.

'May I...?', he quavered as we reached the house. The carriage swayed as we got down.

'Yes! Out with you and follow at our heels', said Julie. There was mischief in her eyes. Also a touch of fear, I saw. She was not too much accustomed to her role, and feared to appear before her aunt as other than that lady wished her to. With us she had dissembled just enough—bubbling with the surprise she had created. I watched deflation in her when we met her aunt, but then that lady seemed to recharge her with energy, her flashing eyes and her large bosom holding court all by themselves.

'Herbert! Stand in the corner facing us!', she proclaimed the moment we all gained the drawing room.

He did not speak, say yes, but merely went and stood head bowed, arms at his sides.

'Has he behaved himself?', she asked.

'No, Aunty, no—he showed his thing. You can see it sticking up, just as we could. Poor Emily and Jane were quite embarrassed, just as you might guess'.

'Of course they were, the pets! Oh, such a wicked, wicked, naughty man he is. Herbert! Undo your trousers, push them down, tuck up your shirt and put your hands behind your neck. If you are to display yourself, then you will do so properly—you understand?'

We had seated ourselves by then in quite grand chairs. The bell was rung. A maid of no more than my years came in precisely as Herbert's cock was brought to view. The girl did not jerk her head nor blush, but stood quiescent as such servants do.

'Wine, Mary, please—the white'.

'Yes, m'am—and shall I, shall I . . .'

'After you have served the wine, then yes. And now, my dears, have you enjoyed yourselves?', she asked in seeming oblivion of her husband—shorter, slimmer than she was—who stood then with his trousers down, his pink-knobbed prick exposed, as were his balls. The servant girl had seen him thus, and had not screamed.

'There were VERY naughty parties, Aunty. We will tell you later of them if you wish'.

'Julie, indeed you must. I am really all agog to hear. Your parents—Emily and Jane—are well? Oh good.

So long as you have both been nourished, then I am sure they will be satisfied. You understand that nourishment does not mean food, for that is taken even more for granted, yes? I'm sure you understand'.

The maid entered at that moment with a tray, and Uncle Herbert standing immobile.

'Shall I now, m'am?', Mary asked. She moved smoothly, had our glasses filled.

'She loves to do this. One day she will marry well', our hostess said. She beckoned Mary and the maid went and stood close to her, head bowed expectantly, a fey look on her face. —'What is it you do first, Mary?', she was asked.

'Kiss you, m'am'.

'And, for your sins, you show your bottom?'

'Yes'. A breathless yes such as I might myself have offered to the waiting room.

'It is permitted, Mary, then. Julie, will you uncover her?'

Her aunt then drew the maid quite roughly down and brought her mouth to hers, fumbling at Mary's dress which she unbuttoned to the waist and so revealed the girl's round breasts which dangled to her waiting palm. Julie had risen and drew up Mary's skirt at the same time to bare her naked bottom to us. All the while came the wet sounds of tongues and lips until I felt the maid was being veritably devoured.

Ringing Mary's waist with her left arm, and facing us with the girl's bottom bulging to our eyes, Julie gave us a superior look and began to caress it with her fingertip, parting the furrow to expose the crinkled rose.

'You may spank her, if you wish; I often do', she said.

I felt constraint, though, at the scene and simply gave a vacant smile, as Jane did also, whereat Julie smirked and put her fingertip between the sweet, plump hemispheres and eased it into Mary's bottomhole, bringing a grincing sound from her which the sucking sounds of kisses partly hid.

Julie's face took on a flushed and puffy look. Her little finger, curled beneath, tickled Mary's nest at the same time and caused the girl to wriggle much. Uncle Herbert looked the more forlorn the more she did so, yet in his forlorn stance, too, was something of a lustful eagerness, I being quite unable to explain the mixture of his sentiments, and expecting him at any moment to advance upon the maid. His prick and nose both quivered, and his eyes were glazed. Julie turned round her head to him—seeing my glance in his direction—and said 'NO!' at him with biting sharpness, much as one might speak to a pet dog. Thereat his face took on the look of a schoolboy who is caught with the jam spoon in his mouth.

'Very well—she may be put to him . . . or he to her', said Julie's aunt, and pushed the girl up as she did, while Julie took her finger out.

'M . . . may I, mistress?', Mary quavered, straightening up and her dress in crumpled folds around her waist. Her stockings sagged and looked not as they should have done.

'You must do as you are told, Mary. Must not we all? Come, girl. Julie—sit down and do not preen yourself too much. He may be put to you as well this afternoon, if not to our dear friends as well'.

The maid was led then by her mistress to the corner where stood Uncle Herbert. At their approach, he blinked but did not move. Mary had a flushed look, her mouth agape.

'Bend your knees, Herbert! Let the girl be entertained', we heard, and at that the simpleton—for I could not then think of him as other than such—placed his hands behind him at the junction of the walls to support himself and flexed his then bared knees, his trousers at his ankles.

Mary's thighs were plump and rich. I rather liked the look of them and fain would have run my tongue around the inner surfaces above her stocking tops. She did not keep her stockings straight, though, and looked sloppy, which was a bad fault. Nudged forward by her mistress, her belly then approached his own with his knob a-waggle at her bush.

'Down more, you fool!' was said to Herbert by his wife.

His hands groped desperately at the smooth wall-paper—then he bent his knees more till his cock was jutting up beneath the girl's smooth belly.

'I will hold him, Mary, or the idiot will fall. Perform on him'.

'Yes, mistress'.

Herbert's wife then slewed one hand behind his head and grasped his further ear while she gripped the other with her nearer hand and held him like a rabbit. Mary, being then a full two heads taller than he in his stricken pose, came up a little on tiptoe and urged his knob within her slit before subsiding slowly and so sheathing it.

Ah my, how that man groaned!

'Place your hands on his shoulders, Mary; that will be the best for you. Should he come too soon, he will pay the penalty'.

'Yes, m . . . m . . . m'am'.

Her face flushed, Mary nested him tight in, her legs distinctly quivering, and tossing her hair back with a jerk of hair that gave her for a moment an appealing look. Her swollen titties bobbled at his forehead, nipples pecking at his wrinkled brow. And such was their posture that it was she who had to thresh up-down, and he groaningly to be quite still. Her breath hissed out, her bottom squirmed.

'Let me finger her, Aunt Hilda', Julie begged.

'No, you may not, girl. Sit and learn. Be quiet,

Herbert, and do not groan so much, you stupid little oaf, or I will bring the birch to you. The maid is at her pleasure; you are not!'

Mary then pressed herself more vigourously to him, emboldened by her mistress's stern words. Her hips surged up and down, her legs apart. Her bottom wobbled cheekily. Now and then she hung her head back, uttered little moaning sounds, but was chided for that, too, and so fell quiet. Moist noises came from up between her thighs. Occasionally we could see his pendant balls.

'Have you come, Mary?'

'Oh-hoo, yes—I am coming now—again!'

'Then do it, Herbert—fill her up. Come, slave, you have been taught to do so well enough through all the years!'

'AH!', Uncle Herbert gasped. His ears were shining red beneath her pinching thumbs and fingers as his cock slipped in and out.

'He's d . . . d . . . doing it, mistress! OOOOH!'

'All right now, Mary, let him splash—and quickly, girl, get off of him, or his pleasure will be too intense.'

Mary's heels tipped higher then. His spouting prick emerged and splashed her thighs, she pulling off and back so suddenly that he spurted his white come over her black dress.

'Get off with you now, Mary. Get about your work'.

'Yes, m'am'. Nose wrinkling up, the girl sped out, holding her skirt up with a touch of maidenly fastidiousness. Uncle Herbert, ears pulled, was drawn up and left like a weak puppet in his corner, knob a-glisten, pendent scraggy testicles. A horrid sight, I thought. Nothing of what I had seen had filled me with desire.

'Papa will be waiting for us, Jane', I said.

She flicked a look of gratitude at me. Despite the protestations of our hostess and of Julie, we departed, leaving her uncle like the stricken chicken that he looked.

CHAPTER 17

'I have sinned grievously to you', were Papa's first words to me when we were alone.

'That which is and that which may be cannot be helped'. I answered. I felt as though I had been gone but for a few hours and that all that had passed had been a dream.

'Even so, I acted less than as a man', he murmured, 'putting you to ransom, as I did'.

'Or into harbour? You cannot be both a man and a Papa to me', I answered boldly.

'Can I not?' His eyes coursed up and down my figure as he spoke. I was uncovered in his eyes, my belly yielding, bush displayed. I knew that look then better than I had done previously, thought to my garters—were they tight? I fancied him to lick me like a dog, puffing and panting inbetween my thighs, but that was but a passing thing, a lewdness that we all sustain from time to time with thoughts that come and go fast as the swallows skim the eaves.

He made to embrace me, but I stepped away.

'You are angry with me, Emily'.

'No—I am not. Far from it, Papa—the experience was fruitful. Very—yes. A gold ring at my finger cannot bind me, nor can charms of words, pellets or speech nor season's change'.

'You have grown up, I see; I see that, yes'. He looked uncertain, trailed his eyes about, gazing at knick-knacks on my dressing table as though he had never seen them there before, then swept his glance once more around my bottom's curves. I moved it, gave a little wriggle to my hips, felt insouciant and careless in my pose.

'And, pray, what do you think that I have learned, Papa?'

'To be provocative, I see. It suits you well, provided that you keep it veiled'.

'With seeming primness, or with simple charm? What is your opinion on that matter, Papa—eh?'

'You mock me, Emily, I do believe'. He advanced upon me, arms about my waist. I did not lean my head back to his shoulder, though, or sigh. The window faced me with its open look. The front of his trousers ventured lightly at my bottom's bulge. I shifted just sufficiently to fret his mind, in sweet revenge no doubt, and thought of Jenkins who had also held me thus, his mind a-rage with private fashionings of incest's seeming bliss. The play had stirred me, but reality was otherness.

'Move your bottom slightly, Emily'.

'No—I shall not'. My tone was cool. I wished to giggle and to scream at the same time.

'How proud your bottom and your breasts, my dear!'

'Do you think so, Papa? Really? Actually?'

His hands moved upwards from my hips and cupped my breasts. I felt the old, expected tingling and my nipples stirred sufficiently for him to feel them through my dress. Would he—I wondered—speak as Jenkins spoke? I felt my mind at a distance from my body, as though I then looked down on both of us.

'Now that you are married, Emily. . . .'

'You think that I have become more free for love? Is that what you now think? Oh please now, take your hands away'.

'They feel exquisite—full and ripe, my love'.

'Yes? Really? I expect they do'.

I would not place my hands on his to pull them down, and so remained, swaying a trifle as we stood.

154

His fingers sought my buttons, parted them stealthily and yet with a firm touch.

'It is good that we should stand here thus', he said.

'The five acre field, Papa, is it yet ploughed?', I asked. I spoke the words as they came to my head. The larches out beyond dipped branches to the seeking wind. 'I shall need new dresses, bonnets soon', I said. My breasts were free. Full plump and firm he lifted them from my chemise and brought my nipples tingling to his fingertips, groaned softly at the pendent, silky weight.

'Draw your skirt up and hold your legs apart.'

'I do not wish to kiss, Papa'. The thrust was timely, but he took it well.

The buds of my titties glowed their ardour to his touch, yet I contained myself within and breathed my breathings with a steady flow.

'Do you not wish to kiss?'

He thought perhaps that he had caught the mood of me—that I would turn, be ready to be coaxed. All hinged thereon—which way my mind would turn. Doors opening that we had only tapped upon before. Kneading my nipples, he then dropped his left hand and assailed my skirt. I permitted him to raise it to my thighs. His hand caressed the swelling flesh above my garters and then, feeling up with almost boyish furtiveness, attempted my bare bottom cheeks.

I jerked and gritted, 'No, Papa!' Reaching behind, I smacked his hand away. Thereat I wrestled from his grasp, half turned and made to button up my dress, perceiving as I did the hugeness of his member that his trousers outlined, tubular and long. His hands clenched, unclenched, for he saw my eyes drop quickly and then raise themselves again.

'You have to obey me sometime, Emily'. He reached for me. Again I stepped away and bumped my bottom at the windowsill.

'I do not, no. My name is not Julie, nor is it Jane'.

Oh, such temerity! The moment hung between us as a silence fell. My fingers trembled overmuch and I could not restore my dress. My titties, rosy-nippled as they were, bloomed to his sight.

'It is not?', he asked. A hurt passed through his eyes. He had not realised all that I knew. I felt the guilt of my remark, a breaking into other places, other rooms— the trestle and the seeking whip, my sister's bottom bared to him, the lordly penis she could not refuse.

And 'No', I said—said 'No', and bit my lip. The door regarded us; the walls were still.

'So be it, then'. His steps were laggard; heavily he moved, touched shoulders with me as he passed. All hung then on what next was to be said—the movement of a hand, flick of an eye. Even a breath, outflowing, taken in. I heard the clock tick. Tick-tock-tick it ticked. Moment of motionless, and no words said. The one who broke the silence would not know the battle's end.

'You would have me in the stable, rather, I suppose', I said—said it to halt him, and I knew I did.

'A married woman needs not such persuasion, Emily'. He looked far past me, and I far past him.

'Oh? Is that what you think? Is that the truth of it?', I sneered, and felt a blur of tears across my eyes.

'Think? No, that is not what I think, Emily. Desire is not so much a thought as an explosion in the mind. There... we have talked of it, and it is done'.

'There was not much to talk about'. I huffed my shoulders, felt absurd. 'All men are lewd, at least I have learned that'.

'Indeed you have? A precious lesson, then. And are not females, too, at times?'

'Perhaps. I do not count myself among them, though'. I toed the floor—began to do my buttons up again, but had got no farther than the first than his strong arms enfolded me and bore me down in sideways motion on my bed, hip to my hip, our feet upon the floor.

'Never?', he asked. Before I could make reply his mouth engaged itself on mine and there remained a long, long moment while his thumb brushed my emergent nipples once again. 'Never?', he repeated.

'Almost never', I said thickly underneath his mouth. His free hand travelled slowly up my thigh, beneath my dress, found the soft stubble of my fur and eased my thighs apart. I made to close them, but he slapped my knees.

'Remain so, Emily. I shall not touch you, though. You understand?'

Bleared was my vision and my will was weak.

'Yes', I assented. Then he gathered up my gown in folds and tucked it underneath my bottom, where it stayed, I gazing at him blankly while he did, and so lay in a wanton attitude, bared to my navel and my muff full seen, his shielded prick a-thrum against my thigh.

'Now I may kiss you?'

'No, Papa. You said you would not touch'.

'Yes . . . well . . . I keep my promises even as you do. Remain for a moment—that is all I ask'.

He sighed a heavy sigh and rose, gazed once down to the glimmering, curl-nested lips I offered to his sight, then turned away. Unable to prevent myself, I raised a hand.

'Papa, you may kiss me once—but only kiss', I said.

He was down beside me in a flash. Mouth melted into mouth; I felt his tongue. It eased between my teeth. The tips touched, but I did not flinch. His hands encompassed both my shoulders, resting on the quilt.

'Is it not pretty thus?', he asked, lips quivering on my own. He ventured a peck at both my nipples, then returned his mouth to mine. I waited for a movement of his hands. None came. My nipples sparkled from the touch.

I said 'Yes' softly, kept my arms alert. His tongue roamed right across my lips. Re-entering my mouth, it found my own. I fought a dizziness that then obtained, parted my lips more that our tongues might lap. Blurred were our words, soft in the gathering dusk.

'My Emily has her legs apart still—wide apart?'

'You know she has. No—do not touch!'

A little panic. I had gripped his wrist. He had not moved it, though, he had not moved. The game was perfect—quite unlike the torrid dreams of Jenkins. His eyes were crinkled and his smile was broad, tinged with a condescension that almost made me giggle at the taut hysteria I felt.

'What?', he asked softly.

'Nothing', I said. I turned my face away, bit in my lower lip and blushed.

'You will not move until the door has closed', he said. I made no sound, but arched my back a little to his drawing lips and felt a shimmering of guilt and love. A broken sob escaped me as he sucked each burning tip, then rose and—walking awkwardly—was gone.

I stirred, but then sank back again, placing my hands behind my head. There were dreams to be had here still and I, it seemed, was still the pretty one who had now learned her five-times table but was no worse for that. My heels slipped, but I kept my legs apart and slipped behind the soft doors of the mind into a doze—white clouds, white walls, that ever darker grew, enveloped me and laid my dreams to waste. Through corridors of dark I moved, a ghost within the still awakened world that moved its unheard voices all about.

None came to me. I slept and did not hear the opening of my door, gliding of feet or knees that knelt. My stockinged legs had drooped, were parted all anew and then I felt first ticklings of a tongue that lured its way up, down, between my cunnylips.

'Wh . . . wh . . . wh . . . what?' I woke to find my bottom cupped, half rose on elbows, saw Jane's head between my thighs and grimaced sweetly as she snaked her tongue around my long-awoken spot.

'*Shush!*', Jane said, raised her head, then dropped it, nose into my muff and licked luxuriously again, I hissing helpless at her wicked toil, twisting my head this way and that and gripping at the quilt's soft folds.

'HOOO! HAAAR!', I choked and knew my salty rills to spill in ecstasy upon her tongue—tip of her tongue as she played around my spot and made my bottom heave and work.

'Come on—come on', she husked, warm-flowing breath about my cunnylips. I mewed, I whined, I whimpered, spilled again and left her lips rimed with my tangy salt, the which I tasted as she groped up on the bed and kissed me fondly all about my face.

'We may go to London, dearest—Papa says!'

'What—what?', I blurred. Her tongue swirled round my mouth.

'To London, drowsy-head. Oh, will it not be just the greatest fun?'

'Oh, yes!' The clouds dispersed. 'Oh, yes!', I said again and hugged her close.

CHAPTER 18

Our sojourn in the metropolis was to broaden our experience of life, said Mama. She also intended it, I believe, as a recompense for my unfortunate experiences, of which she said little but had much understanding. To her undoubted sense of guilt at my ill-chosen marriage was added much petulance with Papa who had in part already restored a measure of his wealth by some fortunate bartering, or whatever it may be called, on the Stock Exchange. Our servants had been reduced to two, however, so I felt that he had not made so much progress as he hoped.

'There are people far worse off than we', Mama said in a practical manner and several times extolled me that, were I able to achieve a divorce and to marry again, I was to bully my husband into purchasing so much bed linen, crockery, and other total necessities that half a lifetime would pass before one needed to spend any more on replenishments. It is a philosophy that I find eminently practical.

Eveline was full of bounce. James had creamed her bun, I was sure of that, but was not so tactless as to ask her directly. There were few enough potential suitors for such an attractive young thing in the surrounding countryside and, once her titties, her cunny and her bottom had been tickled up, she was bound to seek appeasement of her natural desires.

James put on an air of dolefulness and solemnity when our departure was announced. He would not grieve for long, though, for I did not doubt that Mary accommodated him as well—a matter to which many a master and mistress of a house lend silent understanding, the latter showing the utmost discretion provided that her own furrow continues to be well-ploughed.

We were to stay in Kensington with the Harringtons—friends of our parents, it had been arranged.

'They are neither over-bold nor staid and so will suit you admirably', said Mama, which caused Jane to say that they sounded dull.

'As to that, dear, do not be too flighty or you will never find a nest', was the reply. There was much such badinage, but always a merry understanding underneath that we might do as we would, but should not talk too much about it as regards ourselves, though we might do so in a roundabout way by reference to others.

Upon my mentioning that we had visited Julie's uncle and aunt, Mama responded that he was a strange man, and so caused our eyebrows to lift, for we had naively thought it something of a secret.

'Men may be obedient, just as women have to be, but they must withal be manly still', Mama said and regaled us with several tales of ladies and their valets, the latter covering or servicing them when they wished, but with the utmost humbleness and respect, and never otherwise taking advantage of the willing, unveiled limbs unless they were bidden to. —'In such circumstances', continued Mama with an openness she did not normally have, but which seemed in a subtle way to pay obeisance to my 'married' state, 'the servant is rarely if ever permitted to kiss the lady, but...'

'He merely puts his cock to her', Jane interrupted, for the three of us were then alone, though joined immediately after this interpolation by Eveline who sat flushed-face with eagerness to listen to our chatter.

'Oh, shush!', I said, for Eveline had caught the last three words and had quite a look of mischief in her eyes which she endeavoured to subdue with no success at all.

162

'Well, you naughty girl, now that you have said it—yes, he does', Mama replied, and thus set a seal upon Eveline's state of knowledge insofar as she then knew it for herself.

'I wonder what he *says* to her?', asked Jane, and wrinkled up her nose.

'Ah, as to that . . . but Eveline, you really should go out', Mama declared.

'Oh, Mama, let her stay!', said Jane.

Mama shrugged and said 'Very well', and then proceeded to describe in details rather lightly sketched how a young aunt of hers had secretly watched her husband at play with a young girl on the lawn. Being thus occupied, and having the good sense (and indeed, I suppose, the interest in the erotic scene) not to cry out or scold them, she remained in hiding while her husband's valet silently approached her from the rear and—without warning—thrust her skirts up to her hips and poked his poker warmly in her dell, grasping her thighs so firmly that she could not help but receive his salute to the full, supporting herself against a tree trunk as she did.

In a moment, said Mama, the pair were at full bounce just as were the observed ones on the lawn.

'Ah, Sylvia, I have long wanted to!', uttered the valet. Even amid her pleasure though—which was added to by the delightful scene before her eyes—the lady replied (with doubtless panting breath), 'Tell me later, Hawkins', at which he humbly murmured his assent and continued working her, to her delight. Afterwards, she scolded him for using her Christian name, would only offer herself to him bottom-up thereafter and never permitted him to kiss a single part of her fair form. He was bidden to call her 'Mistress' only when they were at play, and to retire as soon as he had satisfied her whim.

'Thus it should be,' Mama said, 'though, of course,

it is not to be recommended with the lower orders, dears, so be advised.'

Eveline nodded, wide-eyed and wide-mouthed, and clearly preened herself to be 'accepted' in the vale of such a conversation. Jane gave her an approving nod as if to say, 'Well—listen to Mama'. I smiled at her, and all was well.

'Mama, tell us more,' I ventured.

'More? My goodness, many were the rumplings—just as many as there are today. One does not fret about them, but enjoys what comes'.

'And from whatever quarter, eh, provided that one's mood is good?', asked Jane incautiously.

Mama pursed up her lips and wondered, so I guessed, how to put an answer tactfully to that.

'Keep your doors closed at all times and your voices quiet', was all that she would say. Then Papa entered, fresh from riding out, slapping his crop against his thigh, joyous to see his womenfolk together. Not unusually, a silence held for a moment, then Mama said, 'I was telling them about young Sylvia'.

Eveline drew in her breath, got up, and rushed out of the room. Jane and I looked serious and tried to hide our smiles.

'Ah, Sylvia, your aunt. Yes, dear. An adorable creature, was she not. So . . .'

'You ought to know', Mama said, interrupting him, whereat he perched himself on the arm of her chair and squeezed her shoulders lovingly, donating a kiss upon her bunched-up hair.

'I was about to say, a very *quiet* lady', he declared, and looked straight at me, and at Jane.

'That is precisely what I told them, dear', Mama said, and looked very sweetly smug at the way that he was hugging her. In fact, they kissed, and Jane and I held hands. A merriness, like Christmas, was upon us then.

On the night before our departure—half asleep, I felt my bed invaded and James nibbled at my ear, urging his hard young prick against my bottom's cleft.

'Go 'way', I uttered drowsily and tried without success to shake him off. Lying behind me as he was, he forced my knees up with his own and brought his knob to nestle underneath my furry quim, my nightgown being all rucked up.

I felt its throbbing and the urge of it.

'No, James', I gritted.

'Yes', he said, and murmured urgently, 'Do not disturb them—they are still awake'.

He meant, Mama, Papa. 'You beast', I whispered. —'Draw your legs up more', he croaked.

I hissed, 'No, no!', but then he pushed my knees up till they touched my belly and, at that, nestled his crest between my sleep-moist lips and, biting at my shoulder, pushed it slowly up, parting the spongy walls until it was full in.

'Oh, James!', I moaned. His cock throbbed red-hot in my purse of love.

'Ask me to fuck you, Emily!'—'No, won't! Oh, take it out, you wicked... AAAH!'

'Mmmm... darling... you're as tight as Eveline'.

'D... d... don't!', I stammered, but the sweetly stinging, burning upthrusts of his cock made my head swim. I turned my neck—our mouths, tongues, met. The sibilant juiciness of our desire came sweet to both our ears from down below. His balls squashed under me for a long moment as we kissed, and then he drew it out, wet, long, and rolled me swiftly on my back.

He hovered over me, cock-twitching, and I stared at him, his legs between my own—he vulture-poised.

'Ask me to do it to you'.

'No!'

I would not say, and yet he knew that I remembered all. The memories of Mary sucking on his penis still obtained. Papa was looking at me, and my drawers were down.

Mama had said to keep our doors closed and be quiet. I had been quiet. Many a girl is fucked in silence in the night—only the muffled sounds of kisses and the slurping of a cock within her nest. And then in passion I drew James on top of me, widened my legs and brought him to my thatch. He groaned. The lips enfolded his proud crest. I quivered, arched my back as it sank up and feverishly brought his hands beneath my bottom as it did.

'Say it!', he begged again, mouth blurting moist upon my own.

'Mmmm . . . yes, . . . all right. Come on, but do it slow. OOOOH! Put your finger in my bottomhole'.

His thighs were naked to my own. My curls grazed his, our bellies bumped. Tongue wet to tongue and all the night was ours, the pumpings and the moanings. I was blind to all save to draw his sperm out, gushing up my honeypot, his young loins vibrant, twitching, as he came, spilling our surpluses upon the sheet until it rucked up stickily beneath my open rose—then sleep, then waking, and James stumbling out into the colder dark beyond. I curled my toes and knew no sense of sin. I had made him do it twice to me within an hour, and felt as cosy as a queen.

'I heard your bed a-tinkle in the night', Jane said next morning when the carriage took us off.

'Did you? I must have turned a lot', I said and threw a sideways glance at her and added, 'I did not hear yours'.

'Oh, mine is quieter', she said with a laugh, but had the grace to blush and look away.

CHAPTER 19

Each of us had fifty pounds, donated by Papa, and folded neatly in our reticules.

'We shall go there', said Jane each time we passed a ladies' clothing shop or some fashionable emporium in Knightsbridge and in Kensington. There was much shouting from the cabbies, all the roads full of the bicycles which had become a rage, some furiously ridden on their spidery wheels by men, and more sedately (with some wobblings both of bottoms and of wheels) by ladies wearing knickers similar to those worn by the sterner sex, except that they were of looser fit and were hidden to the knees by a tight coat. Wildly tinkling bells they rode, the horses skittering and many swear-words uttered by the cabmen while enraged old gentlemen occasionally shook their sticks at all as they endeavoured to cross the crowded thoroughfares.

The house in which we were to stay was a tall one at the corner of a mews which I thought a pretty place, with flowerpots on the outer sills and crested carriages that gleamed in black and purple—some in grey with linings of maroon or gilt.

The Harringtons had gone away we heard first, to our uttermost dismay, but this said by a reedy butler as he let us in, and then a maid appeared and whisked us to the drawing room before we could even get our bonnets off.

There, a young lady, tall and slender with a wasplike waist and the most tightly sheathed of derrieres, greeted us gushingly and introduced herself as Catherine. In the background was a young man, standing quiet.

'Are you Miss Harrington?', I enquired, for she had not introduced herself and evidently thought herself above such mundane things.

'I? No, my dear—oh, goodness, no. I am but a helpless houri if the truth were told. This is young *Mister* Harrington. I call him George. Come, forward, George. Be introduced. He is quiet, but in his way is useful. Are you not, George? Say yes to the young ladies—quite the fairest we have had for a long time'.

'Neither of us are likely to say no to that', said I, but did not smile, for I thought her over-forward and too perky-bright. George, in a pearl-grey suit with black cravat, then shook our hands. His own was limper than mine was. I judged him just a year beneath my age, and wondered at his usefulness, but was soon to be informed of that, for thereupon she whisked us up to our respective bedrooms, saw to Jane, and then closeted herself with me.

'When shall the Harringtons be back?', I asked.

'Oh, we are to meet them on their houseboat, dear. Along the river, doncherknow', she drawled, produced a cigarette and then a lucifer and clouded blue smoke about my ears. Taking the moist tip from her lips, she offered it to me. I sensed a challenge, drew on it, and knew a heady, Turkish taste. —'You frequently smoke? Do you frequently do all things—both of you?', she asked, and threw herself upon the bed and gazed at me askance.

'Sometimes we do, sometimes we don't. I have not counted them', I said, and took my outer things off and cast them willy-nilly on a chair. There were no maids to help one, so it seemed.

'Sometimes is nice', she said and looked put out at my directness. 'I do it often, though—last night, this morning, and tonight again I shall'.

'Do what?', asked Jane who drifted in.

'Ah—I forgot that you were *country* girls. There are all sorts of names for it, of course. Some call it sausage and mash, and others...'

'We know what it is called', said Jane, 'but do not relay it quite as loudly as you do. In the countryside we are covered, mounted, if you wish to know'. Her tone was sharp; I had not heard it quite so sharp before.

'Well, ... George is good for that, and his Papa as well. I am *used* by them, m'dears, am *used*', drawled Catherine, although she looked put out and had evidently thought us bumpkins of some sort.

'Are we not all? But there are ways to use males also. Perhaps you have not found that out as yet. What are we to do then if the Harringtons are not here?' asked Jane.

'We are to meet them on their boat at Richmond, or somewhere like that', I interjected and then looked down at Catherine and asked her briskly, 'When?'

'Eh? Oh!' She scrambled up. I envied her long legs a little bit. 'This afternoon, my sweets. Did I not say? A light lunch first and then we shall be off. Come down, come down—I think I hear the gong'.

Such was our introduction to the town, so much admired by those who live within its smoky interstices, but not so much by those who live beyond and cherish woodsmoke and the songs of blackbirds more than the arrogance of city noise and bustle. I would as soon live in a small hut in a wood as in the dusty dens of Kensington or Pimlico.

The Thames at least was yielding, feathered all along its banks by leaves, stone bridges, idle punts, and towpaths where the dog-rose grew. I liked it at first sight and so did Jane, though it was a fairer ride than we thought along the roads to Shiplake where the houseboat floated regally.

I had thought of it as small—a sort of wooden hut

upon a barge, for we had never seen the like before, and Papa had not mentioned it. The *Tangerine* for some extraordinary reason it was called, perhaps because of the colour of its curtains which I thought were over-bright. The main saloon was twice as long as our own drawing room at home, and the dining room was barely smaller.

'Seven beds it has, my dears', said the Hon. Arnold Harrington when he greeted us, a gold-braided naval officer's cap upon his head. There were fireplaces and parquet floors, brass everywhere and vases filled with flowers. The bedrooms clustered on an upper deck, each with a washstand and a flowered commode. The beds were low and heavy—double in each room. I thought it to be a floating palace—so did Jane. We were conducted round like royalty, then taken back down to a bar where drinks were served by ankle-fleet young maids.

One in particular caught my eye. She looked no more than sixteen and was small but shapely, and with corngold hair. Our host—then being alone with us—smiled at my look towards the girl.

'You may have her tonight, if you wish', he said.

I blinked. His boldness was too much—particularly as we had never met before.

'Arnold! What is to do?', a female voice then sounded, and we all looked up. A lady whom I guessed to be our hostess stood within the doorway, clad in a filmy peignoir that floated down below her ample thighs. Beneath she wore a light, pale blue chemise, and patently no drawers. Her garters were of ruffled purple and her stockings pink. Laced boots reached up her strong calves to her knees.

George behind her stood, his hair awry and jacket off, his loose cravat held in her grip as though he were a pony.

'What is it, my dear?', our host asked languidly.

170

'That Catherine. She is encouraged overmuch. I caught her fiddling with him on her bed. Step forward, George—show your shame to these young ladies', uttered she majestically, then drew him sideways to her shoulder with a squawk from him, whereat we saw his penis, rigid, sticking out, his trousers opened and the sides tucked in.

'Fiddling, indeed! You know how well she plays male instruments, my pet. See to him, will you? What a ghastly sight he looks! I'm sure the girls are thoroughly embarrassed, are you not? Pray do not answer, for I see a certain shyness in your eyes. Priscilla, my dear, will you not take him off and see to him? The wretched youth is overwrought with all these sights of femininity. I will see to it that Catherine has a scorched bottom for her sins. Deal with him as you will. You best know how'.

'Yes, dear—for if you say so, then I will. Come! No—do not hide it away! Your naughtiness has gone too far for that'.

'YOO-HOOO! MA-MA!' squeaked George at that point, for in turning she released the ends of his cravat and took hold of his prick instead to lead him off. We heard her feet go heavily up to the upper deck, his own more stumbling and some further squeaks from him. Her voice rumbled, bumbled, then a door was closed.

'As we were saying? What were we saying—what?'

'What a pleasant day it is', said Jane, and kept the straightest face I ever saw.

'Indeed. Where are we? Henley, Shiplake, Mortlake? I forget. The time is wearisome without the charm of such as you—dear daughters of my closest friend. You have both been tried and put to it, I trust? If not by . . . hmmmm . . . then, well, perhaps by . . . hmmm. . . . As to the maid, yes, yes, of course. She answers to three rings—or is it four? Jenny, what do you answer to?', he called to the girl who had stood behind the bar with her back to us all the time and was polishing a glass.

'Three, sir. Or sometimes four. I forgets myself, and often I bumps into Carrie on the way. She don't know either. She forgets like me'.

'Answer to one tonight, and then you'll know.'

'Yes, sir, I will that. Does the young lady wish me at a special time?', the girl asked, but she did not turn. All servants turn—should turn—when they are spoken to. Papa had birched a maid or two for less. I fancied, of a sudden, birching Jenny's bottom—felt myself to be Papa, and understood a little better what he did.

'Well, Emily?' Our host looked to me, asked me languidly.

I, not to be put out, said 'Ten o'clock' and twirled my glass against my lips. Out of the corner of my eye I saw the maid hunch up her shoulders just a little, then relax. She turned her face, looked shyly, then looked back. I loved her in that moment, or I thought I did, would fluff her corngold hair and make her mew, tickle her cunny, make her jerk while I looked down into her pleading eyes. She would be Emily and I would be Papa, but when I lay upon her then I would be James.

'I shall be with you, too, at ten o'clock', said Jane.

'Of course you shall—you always sleep with me', I fibbed defensively before our host.

Jenny came slowly round the bar and refilled our glasses with a crisp white wine. Her knee touched mine in passing, warm and small.

'You always sleep together, eh, at home? And elsewhere, too? I say, what luxury, what enviable delights, when you are being...well...eh, what?', our host responded.

'Either we are all mad here, or else the world is square', laughed Jane. She cocked her head and asked, 'What DID you mean?'

172

'Ah well, I meant to say—when you are being...
either of you...both. Jenny, go out, please, for the
girls are shy'.

'Yes, sir'. She floated, glanced a shy, fey look at me
and then was gone. I thought of her titties, and a milky,
baby taste. My tongue would lick amid her moistening
curls. The brass-bound, polished door closed with a
click. I fancied hearing George moan above.

'Quite simple, really, for I lie on Emily and stick
my bottom up and hide her eyes. She cannot see then
when he puts it in', said Jane. 'Her innocence is very
sweet—like yours', she added with a luring smile. I
saw she took to him and his strange talk. I did not mind
myself his goatee beard, his lips a little thick, but strong.

'What treasures!', he exclaimed and then stood up.
His penis proud showed through his trouser cloth. 'The
best of it is that I thought you might be dull', he continued in a different tone—one that had settled as a
cow does in a field before it rains.

'No, we are never dull', said I. I thought it best to
speak—not seem less bold than Jane had shown herself.

'He wishes us to say our prayers', said Jane, and
produced from him a charming, boyish smile that yet
showed hesitation at her words. I watched her words
chase round within his mind and come to settle on one
leg.

'The gentleman sits and the young lady kneels', I
said. I was other than the bumbling fool he first had
seen. His eyes showed that. Blue eyes, they were—had
a metallic sheen.

'Ah, so! Then come, girls—say your prayers in
turn', he uttered. Loosing quickly all his trouser buttons, he revealed a member of impressive size. The
crest was rubicond and swollen up. The veins showed
clearly on the stem.

'Go on', said Jane to me. —'No, you', I said.
—'Oh, very well—how boring it all is', she laughed

self-consciously and rose to cast herself then down between his legs. Head bent, mouth open, she absorbed three inches of his rigid prick, causing his eyes to close with pleasure.

'Mmmm!', he then hummed. Her lips moved wetly up and down, causing his cock to pulse the more. His eyelids quivered, then he beckoned me. I stood unsteadily. Jane's eyes were closed. Devotion showed in both her sucking cheeks. —'Come here', he uttered in a lordly voice. I reached the chair arm and bent over him, put one hand down and touched Jane's head, his tongue a wild snake in my mouth, hand puckering my skirt up at the back.

'It's all right—I won't let him come', Jane gurgled down below, and all was fire. My right knee was lifted, poised upon the arm. A gentle fingertip worked round my spot—the other sought my bottomhole. Warm mouth of mine to his strong, parted lips—the sweeping, liquid sounds from Jane's own mouth. I felt him bucking to the sucking sound. His finger probed my rose—two inches, three. I mewed, I moaned. The bar was swirling round.

'Come—let me have you!' Hot against my lips he spoke.

'Yes—let him, Emily—I want to see'. Jane spluttered and unbent, stood up.

'No! Not in front of you!', I squeaked.

She seized my legs and he my arms and bore me wriggling to a velvet-covered couch.

'Don't, Jane, you beast! WOW-OH!'

Laid on my back, she held my arms while he took up position inbetween my legs, cock thrumming on my belly, thick and moist with her saliva as his pego was. I kicked, though not frenetically. His knob slipped backwards through my dark thicket and then nubbed beneath the seeping lips.

'She likes to be teased', said Jane. 'Just hold it there'.

'I d . . . d . . . don't!' I whimpered while the smooth and swollen crest surged at my clitoris. I jittered, wriggled, but he held me down, as most I wished him to—as well he knew. As well Jane knew, also, for then she bent and kissed my wobbling lips and soothed away my seeming petulance.

'Be as you are with Papa, darling.'

'No, I'm not', I whined, and prayed that Arnold had not heard. I could not see him, face upwards to hers. Her tongue curled up between my upper lip and teeth and licked along, and then his tool—his throbber, corker, call it what you may—slipped inbetween the portals and grooved up. —'B . . . b . . . b . . . b . . .', I whimpered mindlessly, then had it lodged within me to his balls that nestled roundly underneath my cleft.

Jane rose, half rose, and stroked my face, then moved her hand upwards to my hair. His mouth mashed down on mine, and I was lost—lost to the strong, thick piston movements of his cock, aware of his trousers rumpled down between us both, a-rubbing on my legs and that a lewdness that I much enjoyed.

We ceased to kiss and pressed our cheeks together as my bottom moved in rhythm with his urging loins. My glazed eyes stared deep into those of Jane who had knelt down beside the couch and softly pecked upon my open mouth.

'Is it nice?', she asked. Her tone was sweet and soft.

'Oh yeth, oh yeth', I lisped—was quite beside myself with the virile, sturdy pumping of his tool, the steady smacking of his balls beneath my fleshy derriere. The insane desire came over me to have another up my bottomhole at the same time. I sprinkled, grimaced, causing Jane to wrinkle up her nose with pleasure, for she knew the signs of another female's pleasure just as well as I.

'There, baby, baby, wet his cock', she breathed.

Her words triggered off another sweet explosion in

my belly and I came again. His balls were sticky underneath my fur. I drew my knees up, threshed my bottom more, and once more brought my mouth beneath his own, spilling small moaning sounds of pleasure on his tongue.

'What a superb fuck you are!', he groaned.

'Yes, yes!', I panted.

Jane was lost to me save for her kisses on my cheek.

'Your tongue also!', he gasped at her. Somehow she slipped it inbetween our mouths—three tongue-tips touching and the room a-whirl. —'GAR-AAAR!', he choked and rammed his piston in my warm, smooth cave up to the thickly pulsing root and loosed his first full jet of come. Jane's fingertips touched at the bottom of my cunny then, the sticky-wet conjunction of our parts, and no doubt felt the huge veins pulsing as he pumped.

'GOO-GOOO!', I whimpered as he came again. Her fingertip sneaked in my bottomhole. I raised up both my legs and churned my hips, meshing my pubic hairs to his, feeling his liquid treasures flow unceasingly within until he quivered, shuddered and was done, ticking out pearls of pleasure in my quim. He nibbled madly at my ear. Jane took my mouth once more. My legs shot down and straightened; my toes curled.

'Oh Jane, Jane, Jane!', I sobbed, then fell into that misty nothingness of satiated love.

CHAPTER 20

Aftermaths in daylight are embarrassing to me. I wish to hide my eyes, conceal my face—huddle my body up and look away, remaining in my warm, pink dreams.

It was not to be, though.

'Come, you sillikins, get up', Jane said and shook me gently. Arnold had already loosed himself from me, adjusting his dress with solemn care, and taken up his chair again.

'Go 'way', I murmured, but she swung my legs and forced me to sit up, my hair awry, face flushed and moist still with the kisses of the pair.

'Come here!', said Arnold suddenly. My feet wavered as they touched the floor, then mulishly I went to him and had myself tugged down upon his lap. Hiding my face, I let him stroke my hair.

'It is best when she is coaxed', said Jane.

'I know—I understand', quoth he and kissed my cheekbone while I huddled into him like a lost girl. — 'Is it best?', he asked me, but I did not answer him— a rich scent of tobacco from his shirt. I started as I heard the door, but he wrapped his arm more tightly round my own and held me cuddled like an orphan child.

'She has been naughty upstairs now with George. It was not my fault'. The voice of Catherine. She stood somewhere behind the chair. I did not raise my head to look.

'That is your second sin, my dear. To be so indiscreet, I mean. Ladies do not refer to other ladies in that way. Your hostess has a name. Go to your room. I mean to deal with you in a short time.'

'Am I . . . am I not in favour then?', she wheedled. I was pleased to hear the shakiness in her uncertain tones.

'You place too much upon yourself and are undisciplined. I SAID go to your room!'

'Oh, very well. I s'pose . . .'

Her sentence lay unfinished, curled up on the floor. He did not turn. I would have felt him turn.

'You will be accommodated later, Catherine, I do suppose', said Jane.

'Oh, really?', the girl sneered, but then her shoes skittered, for he must have moved his head as though to look at her. —'You country girls are all the same', she spat. The door slammed. My new mentor sighed and urged me off his lap, stood up and brushed his trousers down fastidiously.

'Why do you put up with her?', Jane asked, and looked through the portholes, as I thought of them, though they were elongated panes of tinted glass.

'She has her uses—just as all of you. . . .' He paused, looked at us doubtfully the while I stirred my ruffled hair and said, 'That was a jest'.

'A poor one, even so', I said, recovering myself while buttoning up my corsage that he had ripped apart during our bout.

'Then I apologise'. He took my hand and kissed my fingertips. Then his eyes narrowed. 'Even so, obedience becomes young ladies, does it not?'

'I have been obedient—and so has Jane', I mumbled, rather causing him to laugh and assist my trembling digits with his own.

'Of course you have. Now is the time to be while you are free. A conundrum is it not—though it is true. Obedience brings less remorse and makes the stolen fruit taste sweeter. As to Catherine, she has been in domestic rebellion in the past and would not lend herself to what was not unnaturally sought of her. We have almost persuaded her otherwise by now. She hides her indecisions in a flighty way, I fear—makes brash of everything. With George she can play the role of conqueror. His timidity lends itself to that'.

'You have not had her, though, yourself?', Jane asked with some percipience.

'My dear, dear lady would have put her over, but the moments were not ripe; or so I felt. But now perhaps...' He paused and questioned us with his bright eyes.

'We shall assist', I said, to show my mettle both to him and Jane.

'Precisely as I wished you'd say. The company of younger females, willing, eager, yes! Young ladies have a way of wreaking their revenge on others in a curious way. Now is the time'.

'Are you fit so soon? She has a lovely bottom—is that where the dart is to be aimed?' Jane asked, and bit her lip at such plain impudence.

'You read my mind as well as you would a book, my dear. I perceive in you something also of a voyeuse. Is that not so?'

'Ladies, sir, do not always answer direct questions. Suffice to say that there are certain visual experiences that I appreciate—perhaps enjoy', my sister answered coyly.

'And you, Emily?', he asked.

'I said, did I not, we would assist'. I hesitated— having seldom a bold tongue—but then drew breath and added, 'If you wish to really know, then yes, I would like to see her bottomhole expanded by your prick: the opening of her rose. Is that not what it is called?'

'It is called by various names—as for instance plugging a girl, corking her derriere, or more plainly buggering or sodomising her, though for neither of those latter words do I have much taste. They have not the voluptuousness one seeks, nor any touch of sensuous-

179

ness. I have known ladies who preferred it that way to the more normal mode. As to yourselves?'

'Oh, we take it as it comes', Jane laughed, and was quite obviously delighted with her pun.

In a moment we had ascended to the upper deck. Through its windows I perceived the water-wanderers, the boaters on the river's moving surface, and thought of the great apartness of all people, and how what we were doing, and were about to do, would remain unknown to those who moved beyond, so close to us, and how their actions, too—whether innocent or perverse—would remain totally unknown to us forever amid all the ever-changing scenes of life.

It is not good to think thus: one feels strange and utterly apart. In a moment, though, my more immediate anticipations returned and warmed themselves as if before a fire. Passing along the passageway, or whatever it might be called on such strange habitations, there appeared from a doorway the figure of our hostess who had discarded her chemise and wore only the peignoir, held so lightly about her figure that her bosom and her thighs were seen.

The door to the bedroom remaining open, I spied George sitting on the bed, naked as the day that he was born. His penis hung limp and a blue bow of silk adorned its root, as though it were a gift to be presented, though patently its recent contents had been drawn upon.

'What is to do, my pet?', she asked of Arnold.

'I am to see to Catherine, my love. These young ladies had kindly volunteered assistance'.

'They have, they will? How utterly divine of them! You will not need me then?', she asked in such wheedling tone as a younger female employs when she hopes to receive something that may surprise her pleasantly.

'In a certain sense I shall, my pet. George may be put to her afterwards—if he is fit—and by the same route that I intend to follow. If you would see to his revival, I will call you when the minx has had her bun well buttered'.

'Time it is, dear Arnold, time indeed, or she will need to be returned to the paternal fold untutored, and that would not do at all. He is quite *fuming* to present himself to her', said she, and at that she winked at me and closed the door, her voice heard saying, 'George, lie down!'

As to Catherine, she sensed at once some purport of our entrance into her abode and sprang up from off her bed defensively.

'Oh—have you come to apologise?', she asked with hope that faded quickly after one long look at us.

'I, dear Catherine, have come to present you with a compliment', said Arnold, and wrapped his arms around her so suddenly that she had no time to retreat.

'What are you about?', she screeched. Her calves swung as he raised her feet from off the floor and flung her willy-nilly on her face down on the bed, exhorting us at the same time to throw her dress up and remove her drawers.

'No, no! You shame me! Don't!', she howled while, business-like, we gathered up her pink, silk gown and uncovered the most heavenly of legs sheathed in fine stockings of a matching shade, with rose-red garters and—to my surprise—white, frilly drawers when I had expected a bold, naked bottom.

Arnold held her shoulders firmly while we got them off despite her kicks, the strong thrusts of her legs.

'You beasts! I'll tell Papa!', she screeched, arms flailing wildly like a bird with broken wings.

'Oh, Catherine, what a lovely bottom!', Jane exclaimed. The skin was milky, flawless, and the twin globes as round as the two halves of a split apple yet resilient as rubber, warm as toast.

'Toy with her first. I will hold her up', said Arnold

wherewith, to a wild cry from Catherine, he eased his free arm underneath her belly and by main force lifted it so that it poised three inches off the bed, her feet scrabbling to take purchase on the floor, but all in vain. She was deliciously elevated, ready for our fingers and our tongues, her vain cries pealing through the air.

'Emily, twist on your back and put your mouth up to her quim', said Jane—a throaty thrumming of excitement in her voice.

I could scarce see how I could, for my back would be precariously supported on the bed's edge, but by digging my heels into the carpet and with Jane a-straddling me and gripping my slim waist between her legs, I managed the quaintly acrobatic act and lay face up beneath the girl's furred quim while my sister bent and thumbed her bottom cheeks apart to run her tongue around her puckered rose.

'THOO-AH!', moaned Catherine while Arnold gripped the nape of her neck and pressed her face into the quilt, I in that moment sleeking up my tongue and finding that small bud at the upper meeting of her lovelips which extols desire from even the most frigid of females, given she is firmly held.

'Mmmm...', came from Jane who evidently had snaked her tongue into the girl's warm bottomhole.

'MA-MA! MA-MA!', moaned Catherine in smothered tones. In her up-slung position her tummy was supported both by my up-reaching hands and by Arnold's arms, and from the wild movements of her fine, long legs, I knew her feet to be raised from off the floor. —'No, no, no, no!', whined Catherine, but her cunny by then was moistening well. The sleek folds of her cunny parted to my tongue. I sought within and found the silken walls and heard her whimpering as Jane, too, titillated her.

'Do not let her come, my pets. My prick will do that', I heard Arnold say.

'Her bottom is open for you now', said Jane, and at that I slithered—back down—on the floor as my sister stepped aside, though gripping the girl's rich buttocks in her hands, as I saw on rising.

'He can't! He mustn't! Oh, dear heavens, save me—let me rise!', screeched Catherine.

'Fetch the birch, Emily. I have one ready in the cupboard there', said Arnold, pointing as he spoke.

A letch—as men are wont to call it—came upon me then to see it done: to see, perhaps, how Jane herself had looked when being trestled. Had her legs kicked much as Catherine's might, and had her bottom reddened, had she screeched as this girl surely would? There was in me a hardness I had not expected—a sense of that 'revenge' of which Arnold had spoken, though I knew not the source of that emotion nor its real direction.

The implement being quickly found, I turned back to the bed where Catherine was alternating pleas with imprecations all the while that Arnold held her neck and Jane her bottom cheeks, her fingers well pressed into the proud flesh. Was I to swish the twigs? I knew not how to, though. Indeed, there is an art to it, for only a third or so of the bunched teasers should hiss a path across an offered orb, and even so with artfulness, not rage. The wrist should act with suppleness. I speak in hindsight, having learned much since.

'I will do it, Emily. Come, hold her neck. Keep a firm grip thereon—ignore her howls. She may have to become more used to this in future weeks'.

'I won't—no never! Don't you dare!', cried Catherine while my hand slid beneath his own, and I extending the birch to him.

'You, Jane, sit on the bed and ring her waist', came the command, the which my sister gladly did, her legs askew and facing him, as I was with my feet tucked under me.

'I will do anything!', squealed Catherine in pleading, though she most obviously knew not what she said.

'You are going to', replied Arnold coldly.

Taking up position at her bumptious rear, he tapped her with the twigs and brought a nervous squeak from her.

'Don't, please! I *will* let you—honestly!'

'After your medicine, no doubt you will, but pray remember, Catherine, that it is not I alone you have to please. There are other pricks that wait, my sweet, to invade your bottomhole and squirt their urging juices in. Your bottom cheeks will positively bloom with all the nourishment they will receive'.

SWOOO-ISSSH!

'NAR-HAAAR! Oh NO!', came from the maiden then, and I admit to screwing up my eyes as the twigs assailed her lovely derriere, making her roll it all about while Jane held both arms to keep a hold on her.

'Please, please! It stings! No more! WA-HOOO!', wailed Catherine beneath the searching sweeping of the twigs.

'No MORE? Are you to say the same after your first cock, Catherine? You who have taunted, teased, and boasted of that which you have never had?'

'I have . . . I almost . . . THOOOO! It's burning me, it's burning!'

'It is meant to, dear', said Jane, and cast at me over her shoulder a look of utmost mischief, and at the same time challenging such thoughts as I had often had of her.

'No, stop—no, stop! It's not fair! HAAAR! YEEE-OUCH!'

'A labour of love, and all is fair in it. Six for a girl who teases, Catherine; a dozen for a stubborn one. Which will you be?', growled Arnold then.

'I'll *be* . . . I'll *be* . . . I'll *be* . . . FOO-AAAARGH!'

'I find that no reply at all, my dear. Quite clearly

you need extra ones. You must take the cock freely, Catherine, or else must take the birch before the cock. Which shall it be?'

'I will t . . . t . . . take . . . I will!'

'Freely, I said. You heard me, girl!' SWOOO-ISSSSH! again, and a long, sweet howl that came from twixt her lips.

'Freely, yes, freely yes, I'll let him—let you—do it. Please, oh please!'

'Say that you want a prick up your bottom, Catherine, now—say it!', commanded Jane while the girl writhed.

'She has said sufficient for the moment. Ladies, let her be. Release her! Catherine, you will not move except to push your bottom up', said Arnold as we eased off from the bed, Jane moving to one side of him and I the other.

'MOO-HOOO!', sobbed Catherine. Her cheeks were reddened—strawberries and cream, hips swivelling. Her feet had taken purchase on the floor again. She looked most piteous and defenseless, as a birched girl does, yet I felt no pity in me for her plight. Rather did I hold my breath as he thumbed her stricken cheeks apart and exposed the dark-brown orifice between, Jane fumbling at his straining buttons as he did, and bringing his big pego out. Restored in majesty, it glowed its head, albeit showing dried flecks of my spendings, and of his.

'N . . . n . . . n . . . n . . . !', came then from Catherine as the great, quivering prodder nosed against her waiting hole. Arnold then flexed his knees and pushed hers inward from the back, making their positions utterly lewd, and yet with an animality that came sweetly to my eyes. I could see the plum already sinking slowly in her orifice, forcing the rubbery ring and making her fingers clench and unclench. —'No, no, no!', she moaned, but such a petulance is permitted from a girl untried before. Her shoulders rippled, hunched. In vain

she tried to squirm her hot bulb sideways, but Arnold—
already the part master of his goal—had clamped her
hips on either curving surface, strained his loins, and
sank a full third of his penis in, mouth open as he did
so, for my eyes like fireflies danced about the pair.
Catherine had raised her face, chin resting on the quilt,
mouth open in a wondering O. Fair fit to take another
cock, I thought, and wondered if I ever might—would
dare—to take two males at once: one twixt my lips,
the other working in my honeypot.

'Go on, go on—oh, Arnold, let us see it go right
up', urged Jane. Her eyes were polished pebbles, bright
and clear.

'Doh-doh-doh-don't!', whined Catherine, but it was
clear that she had surrendered to his will. As I had
done, upon a different bed, she stilled her hips and
peeped a long pink tongue out as his prick surged up
and buried itself firmly in her fundament. —
'WHOOO!', came from her, and then her head hung
down, her bottom bulbing tight into his loins.

'My god, she's tight—the first one in', he groaned,
but like a gentleman he held it in to let her savour the
huge pulsing of his rod before he stirred it slowly back
and forth, drawing out almost to the helmet's rim and
plunging powerfully within again, each stroke bringing
from Catherine a whimpering moan.

'Let me kiss her—feel her titties', Jane exclaimed.
Already she was wriggling her own hips, as I was, too.

'No! Not until she is more docile and does not need
the birch. A girl should not be cozened at her trials.
Unless she is much younger', he added thoughtfully,
grimacing at his pleasure while he worked.

The sounds that came from Catherine were much
as I had uttered, too, upon the first invasion of my
derriere. At first there is a stinging, then it dies. The
crest of a warmer wave approaches, laps the cunny,
warms and moistens—subtly—the tight interior

wherein the cock stirs slowly back and forth. He who goes like a whippet to his task will never bring a girl to pleasure. The action must be that of pumping strongly on each inward stroke—never with haste, but with a powerful ease that speaks authority. The girl may whimper inwardly—may utter now and then a sob—but pleasure will soon take her if the male is knowing at his task. Nor should she roll her bottom in the act, for that destroys the rhythm of the thrusts. As the moment of delicious crisis comes on her, she may work her hips a little, back and forth, the which will tell him that she wishes to receive the cooling draught.

He will feel her nipples hard, tits slightly swollen. Should he brush her cunny with his fingers, he may feel her spurt, and know that she has yielded to the fleshly bliss with all abandon.

Whether to finger a girl when she is being corked for the first time in her bottom is a matter that concerns as much the character of the girl as the finesse and determination of the male. A maiden who has been ultimately stubborn, not even lending her bare bottom to caresses—one who averts her lips and blushes and will not be kissed—should be pumped the first time, and no more. Only afterwards is her pouting cunny fingered to see how moist it has become—whether it pulses, whether she has spilled. She will then be left to her thoughts, and given a playful smack perhaps, but no more 'comforting' than that.

Silent treatment of such a stubborn maiden is the best. On the next occasion she may be seized without warning and the cock urged up her bottom without recourse to the birch. On such occasions the gentleman must control himself and keep his shaft full buried inbetween her cheeks, holding her neck pressed down until at last she stills herself. Or a female accomplice may at the same time feather her then untried cunny until she brings her on, whereat the gentleman is free to 'work her', as the saying is, and she receiving him with softer moans and final acquiescence.

And, as may be guessed, those last two words were appropriate to the fate of Catherine. Huffing and puffing gently for his part, and urging her hips back-forth in rhythm with his vibrant motions while her eyes glazed over in the spell of it, Arnold released his warm sperm into her with grunts of pleasure that accorded with her own soft cries at being inundated with his gruelly juice. He ground his teeth, rolled up his eyes, rammed it full home and let it spout while Catherine churned her bottom urgently as though demanding every single drop.

'HOOO!', she gasped and hid her hot-flushed face, squirming temptestuously as he at last withdrew the long, thick, steaming rod that left her rosy bottomhole a-froth.

Thereat, with a slight, mocking bow to Jane and me, he exited, I drawing the quivering girl's dress down again to hide her gently squeezing derriere. My arm was taken and Jane led me out, shaking her head lest I should speak a word.

'Silence is golden the first time', said she upon the closing of the door behind which Catherine was left to meditate.

'I suppose *you* were very quiet', I answered, not being able to resist the thrust.

'Oh, I *was* dear. Well—the first time, anyway', she laughed, and left all sorts of wicked pictures in my mind.

CHAPTER 21

There are avenues that lead to purposes other than the pleasures of the body, so I have been told by others many times—they having not the daring or temerity to indulge themselves as much as Jane and I. Doubtless we shall be called wicked, wanton, loose—but if that be so then there are thousands of us in the countryside where life is more richly lived than in the towns whose smoke and general air of brooding clutter throws a pall on all.

The *Tangerine* and its inhabitants amused us for a few days, but no more than that. If one is to be enclosed for long, it is better to be so in one's own abode where trinkets and mementoes, stairways, corridors and alcoves such as one has grown to love, offer a more enfolding air of cosiness, and where each trail and step is known that leads to pleasure or amusement, even to recalling pleasures past.

George I was not minded to entertain, and nor was Jane. There were no male visitors—somewhat to our disappointment—and hence we decided to depart. For home, we said. We were not sure. A cab was summoned by one of the menservants—or the matelots as Arnold was pleased to call them in moments when he proceeded to play the oaf once more, which I regarded as an escape from his closed world.

He was a loyal man at heart. I doubted not that he had grown tired of his rather florid wife who treated George as a male concubine and was not averse to taking one of their young maids into her bed for him, encouraging the pair to take their pleasure while she watched languidly and smoked a Turkish cigarette. He had, though, no bad word to say of her, and benefited much, of course, by sporting with some other girl meanwhile. Catherine was thus upon her back as often as she was on hands and knees, and thought herself the envy of the world once she had recovered from her initial trials—which, in her case, took but an hour or so.

'Father will be dismayed again', said Jane as our cab rolled along the towpath. Two rough boys threw stones. The cabbie cracked his whip at them and was minded, as he said afterwards to 'go and chase after them there ruffians'.

Thus was I diverted from replying to her, or so persuaded myself that I was. The river lulled me with its pleasant sights, its trailing punts and rowing boats, as did the meadows and the trees on either side. Resting my head against the leather-covered surface of the cab's interior, I closed my eyes for a moment and then heard a shout. More rough boys, I thought, in the quick instant that one thinks, and did not stir. Then, however, came an awful bump, a leaping of the carriage wheels and a thrusting as of a great weight against the side of our conveyance. All in that moment I heard Jane cry out and then my head was banged and I knew nothing more.

When I came to I was half lying on the sward outside, my back cradled by a gentleman who apprised me that I had swooned in the accidental collision of his cab with ours. Jane bathed my face with a moist kerchief while our cabbie was in perpetual argument with the other and our carriage door hung open, limp.

'A thousand apologies, dear ladies', was said as I took in my surroundings once again, 'My cabman's horse was frightened by the throwing of a stick by idle youths. I pray you let me attend upon you, for my house is quite nearby. My fellow will see to it that your bags are brought', the gentleman explained, though I took in but little of his words, my head still being quite a-swim from its knock against the window frame.

'Yes, Emily, it is too far to Kensington', said Jane, and helped me up, I being in that condition when one is neither here nor there, but relieved to find myself ensconced in a more comfortable carriage than that which we had left—and indeed did leave after the gentleman had settled with our cabbie who was loathe to see us depart so soon, for he said with utmost wrath that he wanted witnesses, reports, and takings-up by magistrates.

'The nonsense of it. The fellow's cab has suffered no more harm than mine save for a bit of scraping of the paint. The hubs but banged together and the wheels locked for a moment. I am terribly distressed, my dear, that you should have been the victim of such careless-ness', the gentleman declared, and thereupon intro-ductions were effected, he being blessed with the name of Lumley Harrington and being a doctor, as he said.

My head was mainly cleared by then, but I looked pale, they said—indeed felt pale, and perceived our two male companions in that fey and distant state that falls between good health and physical uncertainty.

Mr. Harrington I judged to be in his middle thirties and of quite handsome appearance. His 'fellow' was of the same age, but wore no livery and had an air of ease about him such as rarely falls upon a servant. Being told to rest, and having had my pulse felt several times by a strong and kindly hand, I closed my eyes and allowed Jane to chatter brightly while we travelled on, though fortunately not far. In but ten minutes the drive-way to a house received us and I glimpsed ivy-covered walls and pretty, trellised windows, stone buttresses, and an air of quiet all about, broken only by the songs of birds and some far callings from the river folk.

Within, we were greeted in a pleasant, green-walled

drawing room by the lady of the house who introduced herself as Esmeralda Harrington and was little more than thirty, I supposed, having a look of Spanish beauty, with huge liquid eyes and a waist that a large man's hands could have encircled.

'Let us have you to bed and to rest', she declared, and I—uncertain as to whether I wished to lay myself completely down or not—permitted myself to be taken up to a bedroom where a superb half-tester bed stood, surrounded by the prettiest of things. Therein, without ado, she proceeded to assist me to undress, although I protested mildly that I did not really desire to be un-clothed. It was best for me, however, she declared— took off my shoes and folded up my dress.

'Aha, you wear no drawers—like me', she smiled, and proceeded then to draw off my chemise which left me naked to my stockings whereat, to my astonishment, she fell to her knees and drew my stockings taut, I feeling her warm breath between my thighs. —'What a superb figure you have, such a lovely flat tummy and such lustrous thighs. May I kiss you before you sleep?' she asked. The side of the bed was distanced from me by several feet. I had nothing at which to clasp as then she moved her forearms between my stockinged legs and caused my feet to part while still remaining on her knees.

'Madame, what do you do?', I asked.

'Nothing but good, my sweet. Ah, what a plump cunny! Has it been well fed with cream?', she asked, I teetering with her arms clasped strongly around my thighs. At that she gave a little tug so that I swayed towards her and was forced to bend and place my hands down on her shoulders in order to maintain my bal-ance. —'Stay so', she murmured and, thrusting up her face between my open legs, brought her warm mouth beneath my cunny and began to lick with such divine skill and searching tip that I all but swooned.

'Do not!', I moaned, but knew she had the best of me.

'Work your bottom, you silly. Have you not been tutored?', she asked in muffled tone, parting my lovelips like two fleshy waves with her long, pointed tongue and—at that—cupping my bottom cheeks and holding them apart.

'NO-OH!', I moaned, though not in answer to her question, but at the delicious sensations to which I was in thrall. A cry reached my ears from somewhere down below, and I knew it to be that of Jane. —'Hoo-hoo! What is to do?', I cried, though my knees were buckling and I was being edged backwards, backwards, to the bed.

'They are playing, Emily. Reach back your hands and touch the bed and bend your back. Spread your legs further—keep your knees outwards'.

'No, no!', I moaned, but even so my legs were scissored, and in a moment the curious posture was taken up (for I could not help myself), I being arched right back and so my belly and my quim bulged to her as she licked me ever on.

'You will come in a moment—I can tell it by your quiverings. Then you will better sleep', I heard amidst the most succulent of sounds and the ever-twirling, seeking of her tongue. My fingertips on the bed's top strained, for I could not reach backwards to place my palms down flat, my bottom rolling on her hands, knees all a-tremble at her shoulders, while from below I heard Jane a-moaning and many rustling sounds. —'Come, dear. How often have you not come upon a manly prick?', she slurred from her long lappings all around and inbetween my puffy lips, I gurgling, trying to re-strain myself, but all in vain. The ceiling and the cor-ners of the walls swam all about.

'Goo-GOOO!', I choked and spilled and spurted, spilled again my salty rain into her loving mouth which never ceased to suck and draw until I felt myself collapsing in a cloud of pale delight and fell back limp between the curtains of the bed.

'Sleep now, my little pet, you'll sleep', I heard. My legs were lifted, swung around, and the quilt rolled over me so that I lay in a cocoon and drifted, drifted with my seeping nest still pearling out its liquid drops. A last, distant cry from Jane, but perhaps I dreamed that for I fell into a sweet and dreamless sleep, to be awoken with the curtains pulled together and a milky gloom, and my hostess bending over me, a glass in hand which she brought up to my lips while cradling my head upon her arm.

'Where is my sister?', I mumbled, wine a-trickling between my flaccid lips.

'She had been riding well, dear, is asleep like you. What a joyous coming you both had of it—you to my tongue and she to ... Ah, here is dear Lumley'.

'Oh!', I gasped and covered up my breasts while he smiled down on me and looked quite dashing in a ruffled, white silk shirt and trousers banded with a crimson sash.

'You must take her temperature, my pet', said Esmeralda to him.

'There is no need, Oh really, I am well again—quite well', I jerked.

'My man will have to see to her as well', said he, and regarded me with loving kindness, so I thought.

A polite knock sounded on the bedroom door, and then his fellow entered, garbed much as his master was. Circling the bed, he came up to the other side of it while I hugged the quilt up to my chin, feet showing, stocking-clad.

'Jane? Where is Jane?', I asked again.

'Resting after the sweetest of labours. A superb young specimen, as you too are, Emily. My dear wife here has seen well to her comforting, as we shall now to yours . . . and you permit? Let us take your temperature the first'.

'Oh no, but really, sir! Ah, Madame!', I squeaked, but Esmeralda shrugged and smiled and took herself beyond the portals thereupon and closed the door, leaving me to stare in some surmise from Lumley to the other. —'I d . . . d . . . do not need my temperature to be taken, sir', I stammered.

'All young ladies do, my dear—and more frequently than the most of them confess. Remove the quilt, Harkness, and let us see the form of her more clearly'.

'No!', I shrieked. I made to gather up the quilt more strongly to my chin, but in a flash it was torn from me by his fellow and I lay naked to their view, immediately doubling up my legs, but then my thighs were slapped, and with a horror of surprise I straightened them again, kept them tight-closed, my arms across my swollen breasts.

'Thus she lies! Do you like to be taken by force, my pet? Is it your penchant?', Lumley asked. Bending over me, he placed his palm flat and strongly on my forehead, holding my head down into the pillow.

'No—please! Have pity on me! How can you, a doctor, act so?', I sobbed.

'Sweet lips that cry, and yet no tears? Open her legs, Harkness, and let me try her temperature'.

'Ah, no!', I squealed to no avail at all, for the fellow seized my ankles and held them wide apart till both could see the fullness of my muff and the pink, pouting lips beneath. My forehead being clamped, I could not move my head and so was forced to stare up open-eyed into the smiling visage of my captor. A tear rolled down my cheek, so real did I imagine my distress to be, though knew a sense of excitement that I did not wish to have. I tried in vain to bring my thighs together, but the more I did the more firmly they were held apart.

I blinked my tears and dumbly sought a pity that I did not find.

'Were you not taught to keep your legs apart?', he asked.

I shook my head. My eyes were locked in his.

'And with such legs, such beauteous tits as yours? You lie, my darling. Tell me that you lie'.

'I d...d...don't!', I stammered and thereat uttered a sharp yelp. His fellow had kneed his way on to the bed and gathered up my thighs beneath his arms, lifting my feet. His prick, which had been freed beyond my sight, nubbed at my open lovelips, felt my sticky dew. I clenched my teeth, compressed my lips and looked for all the world just like a frightened fawn, I had no doubt.

'Young ladies hereabouts are dipped first. Do you know what dipping is?', I then was asked by Lumley whose breath flowed all around my mouth. Despite myself, I allowed my lips to part again, for at that moment Harkness urged his bloated crest into my slit and held it there most teasingly. My nose was pinched by Lumley. I could scarcely breathe. —'Dipping, my dear, is thus, to give a girl the feel of it. The cock glides gently in—good fellow, yes!', husked he as more thick inches of his servant's sturdy tool entered my grotto, causing me to moan.

'M...make him take it out!', I moaned.

'All say thus at the first, and you—dear Emily— have said it several times perhaps. But all in vain? Has not a fine cock—more than one, maybe, throbbed in your grotto, causing you to squirm and wish for more?'

'No! OOOH!'

A growl from Harkness and he was right in, balls pendent at my bottom's cleft, his knob squeezed deep between my spongy walls. Then Lumley slid his tongue between my lips and caused my head to swim the more. Much as I tried to jerk my head he held it steady, moved

196

his tongue back, forth while Harkness kept his shaft full sheathed.

'No maiden are you, for you take him full; which pleases me', said Lumley, breathing warmly in my mouth and then released my nose, at which I sucked in breath and tried not to quiver as the big cock pulsed in me unmoving still. —'Such is dipping, Emily, with the prick embedded, but not moving. Shall you learn anew that which you have surely had already? Is it not exciting to be held?'

'No! Stop it! Make him get off!', I whimpered, but my voice had a betraying quaver to it that he sensed. Indeed, he teased my lower lip with his fingertip quite playfully, and I wishing—all despite myself—to move my hips to stir the servant's cock the more so that a tenseness seized me and my thighs trembled in the fellow's grip.

'He will ease it out now, Emily, and then we propose to make your bottom bounce', said Lumley in a voice more clouded with lust, so that I recognised the signs yet could do nothing but lie rigid there, my feet a-dangle, helpless held.

'WHOO!' The small cry escaped me as the servant's thick, long prick withdrew until my slit just clasped the knob. I feared it to slip out. It did not, though—intruding in me cunningly.

'So hold her, Harkness'.

'Yes, sir, that I will'.

'Ah, NO!', my piteous cry came. Harkness clamped my shoulders, gripping my stricken legs more strongly underneath his arms, and with his knob a-ticking at the oily entrance to my nest the while that Lumley rose, kicked off his boots and then took off his trousers. Ah—the monster he displayed!

—'No, no, no, NO!', I shrieked.

'Plough her, Harkness, while I get my prick into her mouth'.

197

'GOO-HOOO! Oh, no—please . . . GAAAAR!'

Upon the bed he leapt. My nose again was tweaked and thus my lips were forced to part again. The purplish crest urged inbetween them straight away. Five inches of his manly tool slid in upon my wavering tongue and Harkness—groaning—then began to work his own within my cunny which already drooled its traitorous desire.

'GLUB-GLUB!', I choked, but Nature quickly took its toll of me. Thickly and sweetly Harkness ploughed his throbbing pego in and out while Lumley, staring into my wild eyes saw what he wished to see and slowly let my nostrils go, stroking my forehead as he did and gazing down at me with quite a tenderness.

'Suck not too strongly, Emily', he breathed, his shaft well lubricated in my mouth. It entered deeper, then drew out, the big crest bobbing at my lips. His hand then moved up from my forehead and grasped at my hair. —'When you are told to suck, girl—suck!', he uttered, wherewith as I choked he eased it in again to make me taste anew the meaty rod.

'She's a good fuck, sir, she is', said Harkness, ever toiling deeply in my nest.

'I thought it at the first. Ah, Emily, my pet, yes, suck!'

I could not help myself. O feeble phrase, and yet how often it is true. My breath spurted through my nostrils as they worked me both, my cheeks a little hollowed in, my fingers timidly drawn to the root of Lumley's prick, his big balls at my knuckles where they swung and nudged. I was their plaything and was lost to them.

'Let her thighs go now, Harkness. I believe she'll take you, man'.

'Yes, sir—she do an' all. Her cunny's luscious, that it is. Tight as the Mistress when her bottom's up'.

Only my feeble mind—some distant voice within

its hollows—cried out for my release. My legs slumped; I began to churn my hips and draw more steadily on Lumley's prick which moved more easily between my pursed-up lips.

'Tell me when you are coming, Harkness, and I'll give her mine. The darling has not been seeded at both ends before, perhaps. Ah! How deliciously she sucks!'

'And sucks on mine, too, sir. Her cunny has a fine nutcracker action to it. Draws upon it greedily, she does. Hah! Oh my gawd, I'm coming, sir! Now, give her your'n!'

Lumley emitted then a soft and kind of whistling sound. I saw naught but the stem which protruded from my sucking lips, but in a second felt the first gushes deep into my throat the while that Harkness throbbed his spermy tribute in my nest and caused me avidly to spill in turn. Their cries I heard—their moans, their groans. My mouth was flooded with the sticky gruel as was my pulsing slit. I threshed, I quivered; my legs rose and fell, then Harkness grooved it deep in me and held, expelling his last heavy spurts while Lumley's bubbled thickly on my tongue and oozed in frothiness between my lips.

Then silence as we slowly rolled apart.

CHAPTER 22

After desire has been fulfilled,
I prefer to be alone, to huddle
up beneath the warm enclosure of enfolding coverings,
reliving in my mind that which has been.

Harkness stirred from me and was gone, giving my
legs a lingering caress as if in truth he would have stayed
and threaded me again. Lumley remained a moment
just to kiss my cheeks, tip of my nose, my sticky mouth.

'Rest for a while, then we shall eat', he said and
with a bow as if in homage went. Beyond the closing
door, however, I heard a sudden, laughing 'Oh!' from
Jane who evidently approached all in a rush. I heard
a kiss—I thought I heard a kiss—some whispers, then
she drifted in and closed the door and clapped her
hands, appearing to my astonishment all gay.

'How naughty they all are!', she laughed and threw
herself beside me on the bed. 'Ooooh, sticky-wicky,
naughty Emily!' Her arms enfolded me. I tried to stir—
felt pettish, but she would not leave me be. —'They
did it to me as well', she said, as though that were an
accolade. Then came another entrant—Esmeralda.
Seeing us all a-cuddle like lost babes, she smiled and
sat upon the bed and smoothed her gown.

'What wretches they are—Lumley and my brother',
she declared.

'Your brother? Harkness is your brother?', came from
Jane. I tried to cover up myself, but twixt women nudity
is quite a common thing.

'Out of the bag the cat is let? Oh dear, oh dear, my
tongue runs loose sometimes, but both of you are such
sweet dears—and *ladies*, too. Come, Emily, dress and

let us be downstairs—provided you are not put out with us?'

'I think you are horrid, all of you', said I, but bore no rancour in my tone, and got up flouncing, tripping round the bed to don my clothes while Jane lounged back and Esmeralda stroked her legs.

'She does not really. I'll wager you have a lovely warm bottom now, Emily', Jane laughed, which caused our companion to rise up from the bed and feel that portion of my person while I looped my arms in my chemise.

'Did he do it up between your cheeks?', she asked, making me wriggle as she put her finger in my furrow.

'No!', I said sharply, but my pettishness sounded silly and I blushed and kept my back to her in putting my gown on again.

'I like to be held down', said Esmeralda, adding, 'Darling, let me brush your hair. 'Twas all a silly, foolish game, you know, and done in too much haste, perhaps. But even so, but even so, to be up-ended sometimes, in a rush, and put to it by males who are not cruel or harsh . . . He kissed you nicely, did he not?'

'A strange way to talk of your husband and your brother', I replied, and was pressed and guided to the dressing table while we spoke.

'You are not really shocked; you would have screamed. A girl should be petted, guided—lured, I say. We do it slowly sometimes—hours on end—until the girl is ready for the cock. We knew you, though, for two sophisticates, despite the modesty of your attire. What fun it was! Oh, say you are not cross!'

'She is not really, no—no more than I', said Jane and sprang up from the bed to ease her way appealingly between my stool and the dressing table. I knew that careful pose of hers as she knelt down. I pulled a face.

'I am', I said. The brush sloped down my hair.

'Story you are', said Jane, 'You always look like this, all flushed and silly afterwards'.

I wanted to spring up, but Esmeralda leaned her hands upon my shoulders, held me down. I wanted to be doleful and to brood, but I could not. The little flames of mischief stirred and would not be suppressed.

'Ho, I am not as you, Jane—why, you let Papa...'

I bit my tongue. The roof should fall on me, I thought.

'And what of that?', asked Esmeralda and bent my head right back. Her face was upside down, her mouth a perfumed haunting over mine. Both her hands were underneath my chin. Jane's head was resting in my lap. I wanted her to cry or laugh. I had committed a dire sin. Her hands lay placid on my thighs. I would run from there, would fly—become a bird, and never speak again. Esmeralda's upstretched thumbs pressed to my cheeks and made my lips to pout. My neck strained, but she held me tight.

'Now, listen to me, Emily', she purred, 'When the cunnylips are puffy with desire, the cock at a full stand, the balls a-churn with waiting sperm...'

'D...don't!', I choked. She would not loose her hands.

'Listen to her, Emily, you must', said Jane. Her voice was far away and soft. Her lips pressed to my garter through my dress.

'Don't want...', I bubbled, then my tongue was still. Full lips splurged down on mine, were soft, were moist. They brushed from side to side. Words burred and buzzed against my lips.

'Thus as I say it is, and often have you known it so, your nipples all a-sparkle, were they not, and bottom heavy on caressing hands? A dreamlike ecstasy is all you know. The cock probes gently. First you start away, yet urgently are drawn to feel it there, tickling your cunnylips to the proud crest, unable to escape the moment of desire, belly to belly or your bum out-thrust to seeking loins, and then when, in the sticky spell, your rose enfolds the conqueror, the tingling plum. . . .'

'Oh, stop!', I gasped. I forced her hands away, jogged Jane's chin with my knee and then sprang up.

Jane rose. 'She was never whipped', she said, and had a proud look on her face.

'Don't say such things! How could you, Jane!', I gasped, yet the hypocrite in me grew insubstantial as I spoke and all but vanished in a puff of smoke.

'Oh, as to that, we may all say what we will. Such things are said, such things are done. The world is not the worse for it', said Esmeralda, putting down the brush as one who underlines her sentence with another sound.

'Well, I don't care to talk of it', I said. The moment would be solemn ever on or would break with laughter. I knew that. Such moments come upon us all at times. One waits for others to smile first. A cowardice? Yes, perhaps it is.

Jane laughed, Jane would. I loved her for it, though.

'If Papa whips you, you will know better how to be', she said. She did not smile at that. I wanted her to smile.

'I shan't', I said and tossed my hair.

'Sisters indeed! And how well matched! Come, children, no more bickering. What is to be will be. I may today eat beef and declare my everlasting love for a good roast. Tomorrow it may be eggs and I shall say that I hate meat. *Qui sait?* Who knows? We all say this or that, and change our minds. The world turns still. In mist the sun looks duller yet behind the mist it shines as brightly as it ever does. I never make my word my bond, nor should you two. Come, or the cook will be dismayed and throw a far worse tizzy than you will attain to in your silly quarrelling. Be as you will, and

happy be the day!', said Esmeralda throwing open the
door and standing there until we passed without.

The carpets all were purple—rather grand, I
thought, and stretched from wall to wall wherever we
walked. In the drawing room, which had a cheerfull
air and was not too cluttered, Lumley rose to greet me
first, affording me a brotherly kiss on both my cheeks.

'You are not too put out with us?', he asked.

I did not answer, and I dared Jane with my eyes to
hold her silence, too—the which she did. Harkness,
as I thought of him, came forward next and bowed and
kissed my hand.

'May I, too, be included in your sweet mercy?', he
implored. He had changed his garb and wore a fine,
black suit.

'There are no tears, my dears', said Esmeralda,
beaming on us all, whereat there came a knock and a
female servant of some girth appeared, a white cap
crooked on her head, an apron stained.

'Meal 'as bin ready this past hour', she said, and
took us all in balefully.

'Cook, dear, you *do* exaggerate. You mean that it
is *really* ready? Well, we shall come in. I have no arm
to hold, but will follow on our guests'.

'H'exaggerates, do I?' Well, I shan't stay a moment
longer in this 'ouse. All ups and downs, it is—all ups
and downs!', the cook declared and slammed the door,
bringing a heartfelt sigh from Esmeralda.

'The dear thing has been saying that each day for
five years now', she yawned. 'Come, let us to the feast,
if such it be. I suspect that it is rabbit once again, and
fish before. The silly woman always will have fish before. You may toy with it only if you do not care for
it'.

The meal, in fact, was utterly delicious. Lumley
sat beside me and caressed my thigh.

'Are we forgiven yet?', he asked and clearly brought some real anxiety into his words.

'Of course you are. And anyway, you did it to me first', said Jane. 'Sometimes it is nicer not to be forgiven, but to wait and see', she added, which caused me to put my tongue out at her, whereat there was laughter and a general easing of the atmosphere.

'I had best tell you, my pet, quite plainly, that I married Lumley for two things—his money and his virility, and in that order', Esmeralda said.

'There are no better reasons', her brother said. His name was really Mark. I liked the name.

'In your case, dear, only the latter would apply', she answered, bringing a laugh and flecks of fish upon her lips from Jane

'Did he apply to you for references in the latter instance, Esmeralda, then?', she asked, and threw a glance at me which caused me to tip out my tongue again.

'My *dear*, the ink never ran dry—if ink it may be called. Being fostered, we enjoyed ourselves just as we might. Parents as such are such a bore—sometimes', she added carefully, and then as if to throw a crumb to Jane, went on, 'Indolence and summer days—even the wintry nights when the fires burn in the bed-rooms—all beget a stirring of desires. Mark being found one day at play with me, his cock a-working in my nest (such *innocence*, so sweet, you know!), we were taken to bed by our elders to advance our studies, as it were. Being a rampant little devil as he was, Mark soom enjoyed himself between his foster-mother's legs, and then the amourous arts were fully taught us. Oh, many a time there were four of us together on a bed, all coming joyfully. Such fun! There . . . I have told you almost all, dear Jane, dear Emily. Now—as to you?'

'Tell her', said Jane.

Perhaps I wanted to. I needed to unburden myself

206

to careful listeners, as they proved to be, and spoke of my disastrous marriage, veiling much, but even so expounding on the naughtiness.

At this, Esmeralda's's face took on a solemn look. Lumley even ceased to fondle me, and took a cloud himself upon his face.

'There is a covenant—a marriage settlement, is there not?', he asked. Mark nodded his approval; Esmeralda, too. I felt I was surrounded by close friends who drank upon my every word, savoured the sugar and the salt therein and measured each grain carefully.

'Yes, but since I have left...', I said, and felt quite lame.

'Have you declared the most positive of intentions to remain apart? No. It follows, then, that the contract is not broken. Any lawyer worth his salt would say the same. A mere interval has obtained that is of itself of no importance, Emily. Your wretched husband first must buy a house, and that you must demand—one separate from his family; close to yours, I would suggest', said Mark, and gave me a most loving look.

'I do not wish to live with him', said I, and put a pout on once again.

'You foolish angel—nimble-hipped one, pretty as you are, you have no need to live with him. Share the same bed, I mean. May not Jane live with you and— what was your cousin's name? Ah, Julie, yes. And your Papa could keep a carriage there—to show authority, I mean', Esmeralda then declared.

'We *could*', said Jane before I had a chance to speak. I did not wish to for the moment, anyway. Arnold was weak—could be manipulated on his own. My allowance would continue. It was possible—just—yes.

'I s'pose...', I said, and then we all laughed as if a huge bubble had been broken and much chatter rose as to the ways and means, and many of them subtle, others plain. At moments I showed doubt—at others was quite bright. Seeing me pensive at one point, Esmeralda asked me playfully, 'You have not committed adultery, dear? There is naught to lay against your door?'

'Why, goodness, no!', I uttered laughing. Lumley's hand returned then to my thigh and fumbled up my dress a little underneath the tablecloth.

'It is time then that she did', said he.

'No, no, my pet, for you would tire the poor girl out, working your engine in her tunnel. Either one of them, in fact! Later, perhaps. Dear *Arnold* need never be told', said Esmeralda with mock solemnity. 'And, by the bye—Emily and Jane—we use no crude words here no more than are used in your own household. A girl is never fucked, but creamed, bedewed, or spouted in. There are a dozen names for it—all quite pretty and acceptable. There are entertainments, as I call them, here occasionally—when a suitable maiden can be found'.

'Oh? Is she treated then as I?', I asked, then added, "Jane, too', as my sister stared at me.

'Oh, goodness no! Well—rarely, anyway. After all, we felt you part of us, and that is something other. Here, when a girl is put to trials—brought by an uncle or a guardian, perhaps (for such they often like to call themselves) she is much flattered, cozened, cuddled even. I may take her first into my bed and warm her up. Then Lumley or Mark—and never the two to-gether at first—will dip her briefly, dip their cocks, I mean, and hold her till she quietens, then draw out and leave her to me once again. She has then had her taster, as we say, and will not moan nor quiver half as much when put beneath her sire, her uncle, or her guardian. Some girls become quite lewd, some others remain shy, when first alone with us. In bed, that is. Lumley and Mark are perfect dears: once in her nest, they let her feel it throbbing deep, but do not stir the rod and never do they come. That first pleasure is reserved for others. If she must be birched, then so be it. I wield a stinger when it is necessary, my dears. Some men prefer a bright-red bottom offered up to them. It makes the maidens wriggle more, but brings them to obedience. We all must be obedient when the moment comes. It is the fate of womanhood'.

'Do they not struggle, at the end? I mean when they are really put to it?', asked Jane of our hostess. Her curiosity hung like a flag upon the air, as did in truth my own. So often the story is the same, yet it renews itself.

'Am I strict, d'you mean? Yes, very strict, when I am called to be. You will perceive, if you look carefully, two iron eyelets in the wall of my boudoir up above. They are placed high up, and to a purpose. Sometimes when teasing girls in bed, kissing their nipples, lips, their nests, I tell them who is to sperm them first, and some—a few—become quite wild at that. I do not have my failures, dears, and hence a wholly rebellious girl is tied up to the wall, her arms stretched up, a bolster pushing out her tummy from behind her bottom, and her kness a little bent.

'Thus held, I darken up the room and tickle their cunnies with a feather first. They beg, they plead, they sob, I kiss their tears. Then finally they sprinkle and hang limp, their cunnies oiled and ready for the cock. The posture is absurd and lewd, and yet I love to watch the shadowy forms. The male comes naked, ready for the fray. Her nipples stiff, her slit prepared, she cries out wildly, twists her torso agitatedly, but all in vain. A shimmering cry, a squeal (for she has recognised him even in the dark), he nests his knob in her and holds, clasping her bottom cheeks and lets the bolster fall. . . .'

'Oh! I can almost see it!', murmured Jane and let her head fall on Esmeralda's shoulder.

'We all can, sweet', said Esmeralda, caressing Jane's firm breasts, 'The act is slow; I will not have it otherwise. A groan, a grunt, and he embeds himself, nibbles her nipples, floods her face with kisses while she wildly moves her head this way and that. But Nature tells . . . ah, Nature tells. At the sixth or seventh stroke of his cock, she starts to yield. Her lips will mew out briefly under his, escape, and then return again, their thighs a-slap, their bellies rubbing up. When she is brought to such a point, I then release her arms. He turns her, limp and sobbing, still embedded in her slit, and falls upon the waiting bed, with her beneath, her feet sprawled wide apart upon the floor. Ah then, the puffing and the panting that ensues, for she is lost to it at last— may even moan the naughty words that I have taught her in the past few days. She is ridden lustfully, is fully creamed—will ne'er say no again, I swear to that. . . .'

Her voice trailed off. Her lips met Jane's. They kissed luxuriously. My thighs were plundered underneath my dress. The long and amourous day began anew. . . .

Envoi

'Esmeralda was right, you know. It is best to be obedient—or almost so', said Jane with female cunning as we journeyed home the following day, 'I'm glad we met her—are you not? Shall you follow their advice? Oh, do! Then we can really stay together, can we not, and you will both be married and yet not. Say yes!'

'Papa will have to say so first, though, Jane'.

'I know—but really all the fault is his, and if he keeps a carriage there, at your own house, I mean... I thought that quite an inspiration, absolutely, Emily. Arnold is too timid to say nay. The constant sight of it will keep him tame and, oh, we can have fun, I know we can'.

I knew it, too: sun breaking through the clouds. I had taken the actual marriage contract lightly—had not thought too much of it and had not scanned the document at all. I thought of frosty lawyers, rolltop desks and solemn words, and wanted not too much of that. But better to be married and to sin than live suspended inbetween a marriage and divorce.

'Arnold must have a separate bedroom, then', said I.

Jane clapped her hands and hugged me as the carriage rolled and sent up spumes of dust along the lane.

'A whole corridor at least from yours, and we will even lock him in each night!'

'Oho, you wicked thing!', I laughed. More bubbles burst and freedom waved its flags. Arnold could be inveigled to become an officer, be sent to India or some such, I declared. Momentum grew again around our thoughts. Mad as they were, I knew they could succeed. Surrounded by myself and Jane and Julie, Arnold would be kept suppressed—told what to do. A role that he enjoyed in any case, I told myself.

Bubbling thus with hope and new-made plans, we made our re-arrival. Ah, dear blessed home whose walls were so familiar and whose many family portraits on the walls looked so benignly down on us!

Mama and Papa were out visiting, we learned. Of this I was glad, for I wished an hour or two to settle first before I broached the news to Papa of my hopes. James bustled like a bird whose lost nest has been found again, and was much put out that Jane and I spent so long with Eveline in her room, answering or fending off her endless questions. Brighter were her eyes—more sultry were her sweet young lips, and I did not doubt that she herself had been well-creamed by now. Indeed, Jane showed as much curiosity about her as she to us, and I left them whispering to encounter James in waiting by my door.

'I am going to change my dress, James, then I will talk with you', said I. My shoes were dusty and I needed much to bathe. I felt skittish in his presence suddenly and made to go past him, but he seized my arm.

'Emily, how I have longed for you', he uttered with that wild look that young men so often have, and which wise young women try to mollify.

'I am so tired from journeying, James. Not now', I begged. 'You must not say such silly things, besides', I added foolishly. I had halted for a moment in the doorway to my room and made to press myself within, but he followed me and pressed me to the wall, hand seeking round my thrusting breasts. —'No, James!', I begged, then came a skittering down the stairs from the servants' quarters up above and Mary, basket-laden, halted for a second, stared within at us, half-curtsied, blushed, and knew not where to look.

'It's nice to see you back, Miss'.

'Mary—yes'.

James would not take his hand away. One knee was thrust between my legs. He grinned a stupid grin at her. I thrust him off and gave him quite a bitter look. He had the grace to blush in turn and knew not where to put himself. I moved away and carefully undid my dress, but held it close together at the top, waiting for him to leave.

'I'll dust your room out, Miss, when you have changed'.

'Yes, Mary, do. James—help her with that basket, if you call yourself a gentleman. The poor girl has too much to do'.

'All right', he said and slouched away to take the linen basket from her hands while Mary and I exchanged such small quick looks of warm complicity as only women can. James in any case was not defeated— only quashed. I gave him a hesitation of a smile, a nod, as I closed my door. James was impetuous—no more than that. A woman learns to fend away obsessiveness, for love that is obsessive spoils itself, and she who allows herself to be smothered by a single male loses her freshness, her alertness, her *élan*—loses the challenge of the meeting of new eyes, new lips, new minds. The cock knows no conscience, it is said—but neither does the quim when the veins throb. Esmeralda had not said that we would meet again, and yet I had imbibed the simple wisdom of her words despite my seeming mulishness at times, and which she well understood as a defense to my desires.

Perhaps I was different now, I told myself, and peeled my clothes off—looked down at my bed and saw the ghosts, the recent ghosts, of love, saw myself lying with my legs apart, my mind afloat the while my body warmed to tickling fingers, lips that pressed upon my own and underneath my slit. Perhaps it was more furry now? Such foolish, errant thoughts invaded me. Were my breasts larger—was my bottom plump?

A knock sounded and I snatched my dress up. It was only Jane.

'Jane, is my bottom fat?', I asked. I dropped my gown and stood all droopy in her sight.

'You know it's not; you seek for flattery, my pet. Its *rondeurs* are exquisite. Are you in a broody mood again? James has been naughty with Eveline, you know'.

'I guessed he would be—and with Mary, too, I think. He had his arm around her on the stairs', I fibbed, and then as if to cover up my sins asked her to help me dress. I would not bathe, I said, until the night. I felt too lazy; so did she, she said, and we whispered once again what we would tell Papa. Or I said 'we', at least. She would not have it so.

'No, dear, you must tell him on your own. I will divert Mama. Just tell him firmly what you wish to say. He will be pleased, I think. You never know'.

'Perhaps', said I. I felt more doubtful then, and wondered how I might begin and how my sentences would form, and what I should say first, and ever on.

'Don't *pout*', said Jane, and helped me do my hair. She had changed already and looked fresh and sweet, but then pleased me by telling me I also did. I put my wedding ring on once again. Jane said it would be a sure sign to Papa. I thought her right. —'If he notices', I said, and licked my finger to smooth my eyebrows down, then put my tongue out at my own reflection which Jane said was the best of signs that I had my spirit up.

'Hmmm...', I said doubtfully. I felt all tremulous at the thought of my forthcoming 'interview'. I had stood in Papa's study several times before when he had lectured me. I swallowed bravely, though, and went down to the drawing room with her where James sat quietly, said Jane had on the nicer dress, but that was just to spite me, so I thought. Jane told him to be quiet—was on my side. I had a wicked thought of seeing him between her legs, to wreak his vengeance. Even so, it would be quite a *luxurious* and naughty sight—but I kept that to myself and veiled my eyes.

I was still young then, after all. I had such thoughts as all young females do of trying to appear mysterious when in reality one merely simpers or looks quiet, and not at all as one would wish to look. The wished-for image in one's mirror fades and is replaced by everyday reality. . . .

'I do not wish to be ordinary, Papa'. Those, to my vague astonishment, were the first words I uttered to him when late towards the evening he appeared and I had inveigled him into the garden by my side, with Jane's quick-bustling help as she and a complicitous Eveline took all Mama's attention.

'You were never that, my dear', said Papa. Then we both spoke at once and I said, 'Sorry, Papa', and I held my tongue, the birds of my intended words all flown.

'I have decided, my pet, that there shall be a dissolution of your marriage', I then heard.

'A d . . . d . . . d . . .?', I stammered. In my ignorance I had not known that such a thing was possible.

'A separation of the parts—the condition of casting loose from due restraint. I have spoken with clergy in high places. Such is possible—and shall be done. The hearing will be quiet, discreet. I alone shall attend with you. Such matters can arrange themselves by force of influence. You have no need to see your husband ever more. You will be free, my dear, be free. The ring you wear upon your finger may be cast off as an old glove is, and laid aside and never to be worn again'.

The brisk, bright table-talk of Lumley, Esmeralda,

Mark, had vanished on the wind. The grass beneath our feet assumed a darker shade of green as dusk fell. On we walked. The gate to the paddock swung and jarred. A rough turf came beneath my feet, caused me to stumble. Papa placed his arm around my shoulders while my questions twittered, nervous and excited as they were. The matter would be over in a month, he said. Mama was pleased. Was I not, too?

'Ecstatic, Papa! I cannot believe it yet! I thought I would have to go and live with him again, and that life would be horrid. Oh, how wonderful!'

'I who was the cause of all the grievous happenings, Emily, have now at least resolved my sin'.

The ground rose slightly. To one side, a small and darkling clump of trees. Before us stood the stable. Its door yawned. Two crows flew—long complaining— then were gone.

'How happy Jane will be as well, Papa. I must go and tell her. May I not?'

I made to turn. His arm still held me firm. The stable loomed before us. Glimmering within, an oil lamp shone. A labourer appeared and made me start.

'I tidied up, sir. Will you need me more tonight?'

'No, Smithers. I will douse the lamp'.

'Yes, sir. Goodnight, sir—and you, too, Miss Emily. A lovely night it is—a fair old night'.

'Goodnight', I said, and knew a quaver in my voice. The floor within was rough, straw-covered. Papa closed the doors and barred them and I stood all of a sudden trembling, then felt his hands upon my shoulders and leaned back to him.

'A fair night, Emily, and one to celebrate', he said with gentle quietness in his tone. His hands sleeked to my hips and held me thus.

And I said yes, said yes, and closed my eyes.

216

Before me, underneath the hanging lamp that slowly swung, was a huge bale of straw—a piece of sacking cast across its width. Nearby was a trestle, and across it hung a thin, black whip.